HONORING THE DEAD

"Hold-hold this," Papa said. Then he covered the mirror in the hallway. He reached in his pocket, got his knife, and started cutting the fabric at the bottom.

"Why you doing that, Papa?"

"Well, folks say it's bad-bad luck to look at yourself when someone dies in your house. So-so we got to keep the mirrors covered." I followed Papa to the mirror in my room.

"For how long?" I asked.

"Till-till after Mr. Bro. Wiley's funeral," he said, covering my mirror.

If my folks had let me go to just one sittin' up I would have seen the mirrors covered and knowed all this stuff I was nagging him about. The Low Meadows rule was you had to be twelve to go to a sittin' up and a funeral. Not a soul had died since I turned twelve.

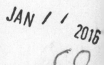

OTHER BOOKS YOU MAY ENJOY

THE SITTIN' UP

Shelia P. Moses

PUFFIN BOOKS
An Imprint of Penguin Group (USA)

PUFFIN BOOKS
Published by the Penguin Group
Penguin Group (USA) LLC
375 Hudson Street
New York, New York 10014

USA * Canada * UK * Ireland * Australia
New Zealand * India * South Africa * China

penguin.com
A Penguin Random House Company

First published in the United States of America by G. P. Putnam's Sons,
an imprint of Penguin Young Readers Group, 2014
Published by Puffin Books, an imprint of Penguin Young Readers Group, 2015

THE LIBRARY OF CONGRESS HAS CATALOGED THE G. P. PUTNAM'S SONS EDITION AS FOLLOWS:
Moses, Shelia P.
The sittin' up / Shelia P. Moses.
pages cm
Summary: "When the patriarch of twelve-year-old Bean's sharecropping community dies,
Bean gets a lesson in not only what it means to lose someone you love, but also in how
his family and friends care for their dead"—Provided by publisher.
ISBN 978-0-399-25723-0 (hc)
[1.Community life—North Carolina—Fiction. 2. Death—Fiction. 3. African
Americans—Fiction. 4. Sharecroppers—Fiction. 5. Depressions—1929—Fiction.
6. Race relations—Fiction. 7. North Carolina—History—20th century—Fiction.]
I. Title.
PZ7.M8475Sit 2014   [Fic]—dc23 2013013838

Puffin Books ISBN 978-0-14-751429-5

Printed in the United States of America

1 3 5 7 9 10 8 6 4 2

This novel is dedicated to my mentor and friend,
Willie Stargell.

You gave the world baseball;
you gave me the true meaning of friendship.

"The axe forgets, the tree remembers."
—*African Proverb*

ONE

*S*teal away, Lord. Steal away. I don't have long to stay," Ma sang as the rain came pouring down on the tin roof of our little brown house.

"Tell Mama and Papa I will see them in hev'n," she said to Mr. Bro. Wiley. "Go on home to be with Jesus."

I could barely hear her words over the thunder and lightnin'. Ma hated to see the former slave go away from here. He had been like a daddy to her ever since he moved into our one-story house. I reckon he felt like her daddy long 'fore he came here in 1935, 'cause she had known him all her life. Mr. Bro. Wiley, Ma, and all our kinfolk were born in the Low Meadows, just like me. Most folk born in lowland of Northampton County died there.

I was peeping through a small hole in the wall at my

mama, Magnolia Jewel Jones, because I wasn't allowed in the room of death. She was sitting in the wooden chair beside Mr. Bro. Wiley's rusty old iron bed. Hurt and tears filled poor Ma's high yellow freckled face as she stared at our friend. His dark wrinkled skin looked worn. His hair was as white as the snow that fell last January. Time and sickness had taken all the meat off his long bones.

To get a better look at Mr. Bro. Wiley, I reached in my overall pocket and pulled out the small knife I found in the cornfield a few weeks earlier. The knife my folks didn't know I had. I cut a bigger hole in the newspaper Ma used to cover the walls. We didn't have money for real wallpaper but Ma was always bringing something home from Miss Remie's house. She washed for the white lady twice a week. I cut in between the picture of President Franklin D. Roosevelt and First Lady Eleanor Roosevelt. They were announcing that more help was coming for poor folk to see us through the Depression.

I saw Ma lay her head on the pillow right beside Mr. Bro. Wiley. My papa, Stanbury Jones Sr., was in the room too. He rubbed Ma's back as if he was trying to make the pain go away. Mr. Bro. Wiley could barely lift his hand, but he managed to touch Ma's head. His long skinny fingers had more wrinkles than his one-hundred-year-old face. His nails were long too, 'cause he said he didn't want Ma troubling to cut them no more after he took sick a month ago at the Fourth of July fish fry. We didn't have much to eat but the menfolk caught enough fish to feed us while we sang songs and roasted fresh corn from the garden out back. Mr. Bro. Wiley never seemed well again after that day. He said he just wanted to be left alone.

"No . . . no, no!" he said when he saw Ma pulling the nail clippers out the drawer. We were listening to Edward Murrow talk about the Great Depression on the radio that evening. Mr. Bro. Wiley loved listening to him. He said Mr. Murrow was a smart man. What we didn't learn about the outside world from Miss Remie's day-old newspapers, we learned from Mr. Murrow.

"Ain't no need to cut my nails again, Magnolia. I'ze working on gettin' right with Jesus, not my hands," Mr. Bro. Wiley said that night.

Then he looked across the room at Papa, who was polishing his Sunday-go-to-meeting shoes. "Stanbury, I don't want my hair cut no more either. My time on this here earth is drawing near. Leave me be while I get ready to go home to be with my Jesus."

Papa never looked up. Never even answered Mr. Bro. Wiley. Maybe his heart was too full to talk. He just cleared the lump out of his throat and kept on shining his shoes with a breakfast biscuit and an old rag. There was no money for shoe polish, but bread could put a shine so bright on our shoes that we could see our faces right at the toe.

I didn't say a word. My heart was breaking too.

I thought about that night as I stood and watched Mr. Bro. Wiley preparing to leave this earth.

"Stop your crying, Christmas," Mr. Bro. Wiley said. That was the nickname he gave Ma because she was born on Christmas morning, 1899. I put my ear closer to the hole. His voice got lower and lower, but his breathing was louder. It sounded like the train coming to a slow stopover in Weldon when it arrived from up North.

"Child, I want to thank you and Stanbury for all you done for me. I thank Bean too," Mr. Bro. Wiley said. It made me feel good that he remembered me in his final hour.

"We done what we were supposed to do," Ma said.

"That's-that's the truth and we-we gonna keep on doing right by you." Papa sometimes said his words two at a time, because his ma, Grandma Ethel Mae, dropped Papa on his head when he was a baby. Papa said he don't remember the fall, but he know he broke his leg. He's walked with a limp ever since and sometimes he moans late at night because his bones hurt him so bad.

Papa said he was lucky to have a woman like Ma since he couldn't half walk or talk. Me and Ma were lucky too. It didn't matter to us that he limped or how he sounded. We loved him, and he loved us, including Mr. Bro. Wiley. As the thunder roared outside, we all knew we could do no more for our dying friend.

Mr. Bro. Wiley was leaving this earth for sure.

"Stop trying to talk. You need-need your rest," Papa said. "Don't thank us. You-you are family."

"That's right. We are a family," Ma said.

I know she meant those words because Ma was real happy when Mr. Bro. Wiley came to live with us after his wife, Miss Celie Mae, went to heaven. Before moving in with us, he lived down on the riverbank in the log cabin where he was born in 1840. He said most slaves didn't know when they were born, but the Wiley family that owned him wrote his name and birthdate in a Bible that he found years later. Mr. Bro. Wiley's boy Peter read the dates to him the best he could with the little schooling he had. Peter and Mr. Bro. Wiley's other eleven children were in heaven with Miss Celie. He outlived them all.

Mr. Bro. Wiley never moved his furniture into our house. Just his clothes and a rocking chair that used to be brown till Papa painted it white. He left Miss Celie Mae's rocking chair on his back porch facing the river. Mr. Bro. Wiley said he wanted to keep his log cabin, along with his furniture. He said he always wanted to keep a place of his own.

Ma thought Mr. Bro. Wiley should rent the log cabin out for ten dollars a month.

"The Wileys gave you that house but all the other Low Meadows folk have to pay him fifteen dollars a month. Why don't you rent that place?" Ma asked him one day.

"I got a head, don't I, gal?"

"Yes, Mr. Bro. Wiley. You got a head."

"Well, a real man always keeps a roof over his head."

Ma didn't say nothing else about that log cabin 'cause she knew Mr. Bro. Wiley had spoke his peace.

Sometimes Mr. Bro. Wiley would go back to his own roof and sit on the porch from sunrise to sunset. If I didn't have fieldwork or school, I'd join him no sooner than I'd finished my chores. He didn't think much of folk going in his house. Mainly us children. Said he preferred we sit outside away from his personal belongs. His home place is where he went to remember Miss Celie Mae and their children. So we would just sit on the porch and look at the river together. It was really named the Roanoke River, but Mr. Bro. Wiley called the forty-eight miles of water at the end of the Low Meadows "Ole River."

One evening while he was sitting in Celie Mae's chair and I was sitting on the stoop, I asked him, "Mr. Bro. Wiley, why do you call the river old?"

"'Cause, boy, it's the only thing in Rich Square, and

probably all of Northampton County, that's just as old as me."

"Even the trees, Mr. Bro. Wiley?"

"Yep, even the trees."

If Mr. Bro. Wiley was as old as the river and the trees, I reckon he was tired and ready to go on to glory. He seemed tired. I gathered he must be ready to go to heaven from the way he always talked about seeing Miss Celie Mae again. He talked about seeing his Jesus face-to-face.

"Here, Mr. Bro. Wiley, take you a sip of water," Ma said as Papa held his head up. Death was so thick I could almost see it.

"That's enough, Christmas. I'm ready to rest now." Right then my heart fell apart as if it were the brown crust on one of Ma's apple pies.

Ma started saying the Twenty-Third Psalm over and over. That's when Mr. Bro. Wiley reached up and put his hand over her lips. The house was as quiet as a mouse. Just the sound of thunder. It reminded me of one of my books falling on the floor at the schoolhouse, but much louder.

The old slave man took one long breath. No pain, nor a cry for his soul. His shoulders, that used to sit high, kind of shuddered down in the bed. Just one breath and it was all over. Over for Mr. George Lewis Wiley. He went away from here. Our friend went to glory. I felt a gust of wind go past my shoulder like the summer I got caught in the windstorm. I knew it was Mr. Bro. Wiley leaving the Low Meadows. I got excited in my heart. I was talking but no words came out. "Off you go, Mr. Bro. Wiley; off you go to see Jesus."

"Steal away, Lord. Steal away, Lord. I don't have long to stay." Ma managed to sing out Mr. Bro. Wiley's favorite song one more time. Tears ran down her sad face. Papa was crying too, so he didn't notice when I pushed the door open and walked in. The lightnin' struck again and lit up the room.

I had never seen a dead man before. I was kind of scared, but I felt I needed to be with Mr. Bro. Wiley. He told me he sat outside that same room when I was born. Because he was there for me when I was born, I was proud to be there for him when he took his last breath. It was the right thing to do.

I wasn't standing there long before Ma and Papa heard me crying.

Ma turned around while Papa watched over Mr. Bro. Wiley. She held her chest as if her heart might jump out and roll on the floor. Then she rubbed her belly that was filled with baby; a baby that no one bothered to tell me a thing about. Low Meadows folk never said a word when a woman was gonna have a baby. Not one word. Maybe they think us children don't know where babies come from. You just go to school or the fields one day, and when you come home, a new baby's living in your house. It was a shame 'fore God to keep a secret about a baby that had my blood in their veins.

I took my mind off the secret baby and looked at Ma. I tried to catch my breath and stop the tears from rolling down my face. The lightnin' struck so low that I thought it was coming through the window. The whole room lit up again. I could see Ma's swollen eyes as she stood up.

"Go back, Stanbury Jr. Go back. Death done come for Mr. Bro. Wiley. Go back, child." Ma never called me Stanbury Jr., unless she was upset. Papa didn't say a word. He never turned around. He wrapped Mr. Bro. Wiley's body up real slow with the white bedsheet. Ma sat down in the chair so hard that I heard a thump. I walked backward into the hall and closed the door. I looked at the president and first lady torn apart on the newspaper. Torn apart just like my heart.

"Good-bye, my friend," Papa said.

"Rest on, Mr. Bro. Wiley. Rest on!" Ma cried out.

Papa reached across his body and grabbed Ma's hand. They were quiet for a while. Then Papa said, "I best-best go out to town and get Joe Gordon to pick up the body."

"Wait till morning, Husband. I want Mr. Bro. Wiley

9

to stay here tonight. Let him stay home. Besides the weather is too bad for you to go outside."

Ma turned her whole body towards the window.

"I reckon it's a good night for dying. My mama used to say when it rains this hard, the Lord is washing a soul to hev'n."

"I-I believe that, Wife. I truly do. I need to check on Bean. Will you be all right for a minute?" Papa kissed her on her cheek as she nodded her head. Ma never stopped studying the rain carrying Mr. Bro. Wiley to hev'n. Papa didn't mention going to the colored undertaker again as he came in the hallway. He pulled me close to his chest. Close to his heart. His voice was sad.

"We've done all-all we can for Mr. Bro. Wiley on this side of the mountain."

"I know, Papa."

"It's late. You go on to-to bed."

"Please, let me stay out here. I want to be near y'all. Please!"

Papa didn't argue with me. He was too sad and he knew I was hurting all the way to my bones.

"Fine. Get-get your quilt. You can sleep out here if it makes you feel better. I will leave the door open, but do not-not come in Mr. Bro. Wiley's room. It's filled with death."

"I ain't scared, Papa. I ain't scared of death."

"This is grown folks' business, child. You will see him when the time come for the funeral, but not now."

Then Papa turned around and went back inside.

"Bean will be all right, Wife," Papa told Ma.

"Poor child. He loved Mr. Bro. Wiley," she said with her gaze still fixed on the window.

They cried together. Then Ma began shouting till she couldn't shout no more. Up and down she jumped just as the folk do at Sandy Branch Baptist Church on Sunday morning. She stomped her feet. Up in the air her hands went.

Then she cried.

Sang.

Shouted.

Cried.

Sang.

Shouted.

There was nothing I could do for Ma, so I lay down beside the door just in case my papa needed me to get her a glass of water. Papa lay on the floor on the right side of the bed.

"Please come on down here with me, Wife." Ma didn't move. She kept sitting in the chair, watching the storm. Every now and then she would stand up and stomp her feet.

"Thank you, Jesus! Thank you for the life of Mr. Bro.

Wiley," she said. As I watched Ma carrying on, I thought about how upset all the Low Meadows folk would be when word got out that our friend was gone.

Now, if Miss Lottie Pearl Cofield was at the house when death knocked on the door, it would have been a mess as sho' as you born. She was Ma's best friend and our neighbor that lived right up the road on Stony Hill. Stony Hill wasn't a real big hill, just high enough for me and my best friend, Pole, to slide down when the snow came each winter.

Pole is Miss Lottie Pearl and her husband Mr. Jabo Cofield's youngest child. Their only son, Willie, is a porter for the railroad and lives up North in a place called Chicago. Pole's real name is Martha Rose, but we called her Pole because she didn't have no meat on her bones. Skinny as she can be. Skinny as one of them poles in our string bean patch in the backyard. I didn't care nothing about Pole being skinny though. She been my friend all our days on this earth and that's why they nicknamed me Bean. Folk in Low Meadows said me and Pole act as if we couldn't live without each other. Mr. Bro. Wiley said we stick together the way a bean vine stick to a pole. Mr. Jabo thought that was some kind of funny, so he decided we were officially Bean and Pole.

He was Papa's best friend. Papa said you could search the world over and you wouldn't find a better man than

Jabo Cofield. He was quiet and gentle. I never heard him raise his voice in my whole life.

Miss Lottie Pearl was the closest thing Ma had to a sister 'cause all her sisters dead and gone, except the baby girl, Aunt Juanita, who lived up North. Everybody knew they weren't really sisters. Ma was a pretty woman, and Miss Lottie Pearl was not fit to look at. She had a long nose with a lump on it and her skin just as rough as a potato sack. She had good hair, but she was shaped up like a man. I reckon the worst thing of all about Miss Lottie Pearl was she talked too much to be a so-called Christian. She would say "Amen" every time the preacher opened his mouth, but she talked about folk before she got outside the church good. She had ugly ways.

Yes, a blind man could see that Miss Lottie Pearl and Ma didn't have the same blood running in their veins, but they surely loved each other. They both loved Mr. Bro. Wiley too. We all loved him. We loved him because he treated us as if we were his children and grandchildren. Nobody in the Low Meadows made one move without getting advice from the old slave man. Folk asked him how to heal the sick and folk talked to him about the dead. Mr. Bro. Wiley taught us children to fish and put us in our place when we forgot our home training. He taught the menfolk to coon hunt and he taught the women how to make molasses cakes. Even

Miss Lottie Pearl admitted she couldn't out-cook the old slave man.

I peeped in the room filled with death one more time and wondered who would break the news to Ma's best friend. I suppose she felt she could do no more for Mr. Bro. Wiley, so Ma finally lay on the floor beside Papa, where they slept all night.

Lord have mercy! I knew Ma would do some shouting with Miss Lottie Pearl when she got word that Mr. Bro. Wiley had met his Maker.

Two

C ome Saturday morning, Ma and Papa woke up
at five thirty just like they always did. I was still
lying in the hallway when they walked past me. I pre-
tended to be asleep because I wanted to hear them talk
about the funeral plans. I wanted to know when they
would have the sittin' up for Mr. Bro. Wiley. Papa went
on the porch to get some water for them to wash up.
Then they disappeared into the bedroom. When they
came out Ma headed to the kitchen. She was wearing
a black dress. Papa had on his Sunday-go-to-meeting
white shirt and the black pants to the only suit he had
in the world. I closed my eyes again when Papa turned
towards me.

When I peeped, I saw Papa carrying some of the
dead folk fabric that Mr. Joe Gordon's wife, Mrs. Duvall

Gordon, gave Ma. Mrs. Gordon was always giving the women on Low Meadows Lane leftover funeral fabric. I appreciated her kindness, but I wanted her to keep the fabric they used to line the caskets with. Ma used that dead folk fabric for everything. She made curtains, clothes, and tablecloths with it. You name it.

"What you gonna do with the dead folk fabric?" I asked Papa as I jumped to my feet, wiping the sleep from my eyes.

Instead of giving me an answer, he handed me one end of the fabric.

"Hold-hold this," Papa said. Then he covered the mirror in the hallway. He reached in his pocket, got his knife, and started cutting the fabric at the bottom.

"Why you doing that, Papa?"

"Well, folks say it's bad-bad luck to look at yourself when someone dies in your house. So-so we got to keep the mirrors covered." I followed Papa to the mirror in my room.

"For how long?" I asked.

"Till-till after Mr. Bro. Wiley's funeral," he said, covering my mirror.

If my folks had let me go to just one sittin' up I would have seen the mirrors covered and knowed all this stuff I was nagging him about. The Low Meadows rule was you had to be twelve to go to a sittin' up and a funeral. Not a soul had died since I turned twelve.

"How am I gonna get dressed if I can't see myself?"

"Just-just wash up and put your clothes on, Bean. I want you-you to look out for your ma while I go to town to get Joe Gordon."

"Yes, sir." I didn't say nothing else 'cause Papa's light brown eyes were filled with tears just saying Mr. Bro. Wiley's name. He tried to hold up but water was already running down his dark face and gray mustache.

I followed Papa to the back porch, where he covered the mirror that he used for shaving each morning. I watched and wondered how in the world he was gonna shave with no mirror.

"Pump you-you some bathwater and come to breakfast," Papa said as he disappeared into the kitchen.

"Good morning, Mama," I said as I walked past her, holding my face tub.

"Mornin', Bean. You all right this morning?"

"I feel sad in my heart, Ma. Real sad."

"Death is a sad thing, child," Ma said.

I went to my room to wash up. I put on my Saturday clothes since Papa told me I would be staying home with Ma and not working in the field. We always worked till the clock struck twelve on Saturdays.

But when I got back to the kitchen, Mama made an announcement.

"Husband, soon as y'all eat breakfast I want you and Bean to go get Mr. Gordon."

"Wife, I-I ain't leaving you here by yourself." Mama kept on taking the hot biscuits out the pan and putting them on my plate with one egg and two pieces of fatback from the hog we killed last winter.

"You hear me, Wife? I-I ain't leaving you here by yourself."

"Mr. Bro. Wiley is gone to be with the Lord. I ain't scared of the dead. Now, take Bean with you. He'll be thirteen come December. It's due time that he learned the ways of a Low Meadows man. We bury our own. Bean needs to know what to do when death comes for us."

I could hardly eat after Ma mentioned dying. That would hurt worse than anything in the world, including losing Mr. Bro. Wiley.

After Ma said her piece, we ate in silence. She wept from time to time. As soon as my belly was full, I started cleaning off the table. I wanted to be ready when Papa got his last piece of fatback in his mouth. I somehow felt grown up because I was going along with Papa.

Ma kissed me good-bye as I walked onto the porch where Mr. Bro. Wiley would sit after breakfast. She gave

Papa a kiss right on the lips, and he walked out the door. That tickled him. My papa loved Ma and they loved me. Together we shared our love with Mr. Bro. Wiley. I felt sad knowing I was leaving him in the house dead, but I still had my folks.

Ma stood in the door watching me and Papa walk down to the barn to hook Mule Bennett to the wagon. Mr. Bro. Wiley gave Papa that mule when he moved in with us.

"Why you giving me your mule?" Papa asked Mr. Bro. Wiley.

"That's my rent, boy."

"You-you know good and well you don't owe us no rent."

"Ain't nothing free in this world, Stanbury Jones. Don't you ever forget that. Ain't nothing free."

Nobody argued with Mr. Bro. Wiley, so Mule Bennett belonged to Papa from that day on.

Mule Bennett was old and couldn't do much field-work, but he could get us to town and back. That morning when I opened the barn door, Papa's mule never raised his head. He just kicked his left leg like he was mad or hurting inside.

"Papa, Mule Bennett looks some kind of sad. You think he know Mr. Bro. Wiley is dead?"

"Don't know, Son. He-he might. Mules are smarter

than us humans give them credit. They love their owners and this here mule knew he belonged to Mr. Bro. Wiley long before he belonged to me."

"I think we should leave Mule Bennett and take the truck. Surely Mr. Thomas wouldn't mind," I said. Thomas Wiley was the white man Papa worked for. Mr. Thomas got the same last name as Mr. Bro. Wiley 'cause his grandpa owned the ole slave man and all of his kinfolk during slavery time. He claimed he thought so much of my daddy but he didn't let him drive that truck unless it was for Low Meadows work.

"No, Son, it ain't all right for us to use Mr. Thomas's truck. I give-give Mr. Thomas my word that I only-only use his truck when I'm working. A man's word-word is all he got. Mule-Mule Bennett will be fine.

"Ain't that right?" Papa asked the mule like he was going to answer.

While Papa was talking, I stared down at the riverbank and thought about Mr. Bro. Wiley in heaven with his kinfolk—the kinfolk that were buried at the river. It's 'bout twenty graves down there. Us Low Meadows folk call the spot under the willow trees "Slave Grave." Most of the graves got the name "Wiley" carved on them. Some have nothing at all. Mr. Bro. Wiley told me that everybody buried down at the river are his kinfolk and he knows who is buried where. Sometimes when he was feeling good, me and Mr. Bro. Wiley would go to the riverbank just to look at the graves. If Pole saw us, she would come running down Stony Hill.

Mr. Bro. Wiley held his walking stick with one hand and my shoulder with the other. Pole walked in front of us, carrying his spit cup. I don't know why Mr. Bro. Wiley carried that cup with him 'cause he never chewed 'bacco at Slave Grave. He said the riverbank was holy ground. That meant no drinking, no smoking, and no chewing 'bacco.

He would point to the biggest rock that was stuck deep in the ground. No headstone, just a rock.

"My grandpappy buried over yonder right beside the pecan tree," Mr. Bro. Wiley would say in a sad but strong voice. We walked on. "My mammy over yonder next to Cousin Paul."

Them yellow eyes that I reckon used to be white would fill all the way up with tears. Pole's eyes would fill with tears too. I would stick my chest out real far to show Mr. Bro. Wiley my strength. I had to be strong for him and Pole. Before we could take another step, tears were all the way down to Mr. Bro. Wiley's white shirt that he wore under his bibbed overalls.

"Don't cry," Pole said, standing on her tiptoes to wipe his tears away. Pole thought the world of Mr. Bro. Wiley, just like the rest of us did.

"I'm all right, gal. I have seen the worst of times. This ain't gonna kill me."

When we were done walking in the Slave Grave, we would go back to Mr. Bro. Wiley's house and help him sit down in Miss Celie Mae's chair. Me and Pole would sit on the stoop and look at Ole River.

We would throw rocks across the water. Pole was always trying to throw her rock the farthest. I knew she was smarter than I would ever tell her, but that didn't make her the best rock thrower. Just sassy is what she was at the end of the day. She asked a million questions too.

"Why the river make you so sad?" Pole asked Mr. Bro. Wiley on one of our trips.

"That ain't just any river, gal. It is my people's final resting place."

"But I thought they was all buried under the rocks?" Pole directed her bright gaze into Mr. Bro. Wiley's tear-filled eyes to get all the truth out of him. That was just her way. She wanted the details, because she said she was gonna be a doctor one day and doctors knew everything according to her. I wanted to be a lawyer, so I tried to be a good listener too, mainly when Mr. Bro. Wiley was talking.

"Children, this is your home now, but when I was your age it was a plantation. During slavery, my kinfolk tried to get away from here. Tried to get to freedom. Late at night, slaves would try to make their escape.

They wanted freedom so bad they'd try to swim across Ole River. If they could make it to the other side, they thought they could get to the main road and go north."

"Then what happened? What happened to your people?" Pole focused in like she had a surgical knife on a patient.

"Well some made it across the river. Some didn't. My folks would rather be dead than be slaves. If they got caught trying to make it to freedom, they would swim to the middle of that wide river and drown. Ole River would pull them to the bottom like it was waiting for them. Take them right on to their resting place."

Pole did some crying when he told us that. I tried to hold back my tears, but I cried too.

"It's all right, children. It's a fine day when a colored man gets to die on his own terms," he said.

I looked towards Ole River and Slave Grave while Papa finished hitching the wagon. Seem like I could see Mr. Bro. Wiley and all his people gathered there. I thought about what he told me and Pole. The white folk had surely mistreated his family. They didn't belong at the bottom of the river. I was kind of mad for a minute. Then I thought about how happy Mr. Bro. Wiley must be when he saw his mama, pappy, and Miss Celie Mae face-to-face in heaven.

THREE

apa, I want to spend them final hours with Mr. Bro. Wiley just like the grown folk. I want to go to the sittin' up."

"I reckon you-you old enough. You are about to be a teenager. Them years went by so fast," Papa said as we headed out of the yard. "Low-Low Meadows men take care of our own—the living and the-the dead. Your ma's right. It's time you learn how to take care of the dead. I won't always be here."

I tried not to listen to Papa talk about not being around. I just couldn't think about him dying after watching Mr. Bro. Wiley leave us the night before.

"Well, I think it's only right that Pole come to the sittin' up too," I said.

"Yeah, Pole too. If her folk-folk say it's all right."

Ain't no way in the world I wanted to go to my first sittin' up without Pole. We'd done everything together all our lives since I didn't have no sisters and brothers. Willie was so much older than Pole that she barely knew him. Pole was surely the sassiest girl in our school and smart too. Most of all she was my best friend in the world.

Sometimes, I tried to sneak away to do stuff with the menfolk, but not my first sittin' up. Pole had to be with me. It wasn't gonna be easy to tell her that our Mr. Bro. Wiley was gone to glory.

I looked back at the house where Ma was still standing in the kitchen door.

Papa threw her another kiss as he turned Mule Bennett towards Stony Hill.

"Why we headed to Stony Hill?" I asked.

"'Cause-'cause, Son, I got to-to get Lottie Pearl. I heard what your ma said, but we-we can't leave her alone with Mr. Bro. Wiley. Up-up, Mule Bennett, climb up," Papa said.

"How long do you reckon she gonna be sad?" I asked. I really wondered how long we all would grieve for Mr. Bro. Wiley.

"Son, you can't put-put no time on a grief. Death is a heartbreak that will keep you up at night. Wife will heal by and by. We all will."

When Mule Bennett finally made it up Stony Hill,

I could see Miss Lottie Pearl sweeping her wide front porch. A slight breeze had a hold of her big flowered beige dress. She wore that dress to the field every day.

Pole was in the yard, picking up sticks that the storm left behind. Even in her field clothes, she looked pretty. Her white blouse was always ironed and her little denim britches were rolled up neatly around her ankles. The future doctor had on a pair of Mr. Jabo's gloves to protect the hands that she swore would be those of a surgeon one day.

Pole was always helping her mama keep their home place clean. The Cofields' house belonged to Mr. Thomas as did all the houses in the Low Meadows. They worked for him like all coloreds who lived on his land had to do. Their house had the highest porch I had ever seen. Papa said Mr. Thomas built the porch high off the ground 'cause he was scared of the water. He had stayed there one year and then he said the water was still too close for his comfort. He said he got tired of the storms that came often. He asked Papa about moving in the nice house first, but we couldn't live there with all those steps and Papa's bad leg. Happy to leave their old stack down at the river, the Cofields moved in that winter Mr. Thomas took his family and moved out to town with the rest of the white folk. He took everybody except his boy,

Christian. They didn't get along worth a nickel because Mr. Thomas said his son was lazy. Mr. Thomas gave him a little house across the road from us and went on about his business. Christian Wiley was the only white person left in the Low Meadows.

I waved at the womenfolk when we got closer.

"Mornin', Lottie Pearl. Mornin', Pole. Have-have Jabo left for the 'bacco field yet?" Papa asked.

"Lord, yeah. Jabo been gone. The ground so wet he told me and Pole to wait awhile. Why ain't you in the field?" Then Miss Lottie Pearl stopped her sweeping. She dropped her broom and raised her hand over her eyes to block the sun that had finally stopped hiding behind the clouds. She walked to the end of the porch and looked at Papa.

"Stanbury, is that death I see in your eyes?"

"It-it is death, Lottie Pearl. Mr. Bro. Wiley went on to glory last night. I wanted to catch you 'fore you went to the field. Need you-you to go up to the house with Wife, while I get Joe Gordon."

"My Lord, my God!" Miss Lottie Pearl yelled out. She threw her arms in the air. She shouted like she saw Jesus coming down Low Meadows Lane to take *her* to heaven. Pole threw the gloves to the ground and rushed to her mama's side.

I wanted to get down from the wagon to hug the women but I had to take care of the menfolk business with my papa.

"Lottie Pearl, it-it gonna be all right. Mr. Bro. Wiley was old and tired of this here earth," Papa said. "He was ready to go on home."

"Lord Jesus. I should have known he was gone. Last night I dreamed I was lost in this big house. That's a sho' sign of death," she said.

While Miss Lottie Pearl was talking, I reckon the Holy Ghost got hold of Pole because she stomped her feet a few times like she wanted to shout. Her big pony-tails went up and down and she was doing some crying. It hurt me to my heart to see her broke up that way.

It took them a few minutes, but the womenfolk pulled themselves together and wiped the tears from their eyes.

"You all can leave. I'll take care of Mama," Pole assured us as they held hands.

"Yes, Stanbury, Pole is right. Y'all go on." Miss Lottie Pearl paused and walked back to the edge of the porch. "Would you please ask Mrs. Gordon to call Pullman Railroad in Chicago for me? Tell them to get word to Willie that Mr. Bro. Wiley is dead," she said. "He pay half price for train tickets and he sho' gonna want to come South for the funeral."

"I'll make sure she calls for you," Papa told our

neighbor. It sure would be nice for Willie to come to the funeral. He always brought me and Pole candy that the porters pass out on the train. Most of all he had stories from all over the country to tell us. We could travel with Willie without even leaving the front porch.

I wondered what Mrs. Gordon would say to them important white folk up in Chicago. In school we read all about George Pullman's first sleeping car carrying the body of President Lincoln from Washington. We learned about how all the coloreds that worked for George Pullman Company were also called "George" by the white passengers, even after he died.

"Pole, come on in this house and put your Saturday clothes on 'cause we got to go see 'bout Sister."

Miss Lottie Pearl turned to walk in the house then.

"Lord have mercy, Jesus," she told the Lord as Pole followed her inside.

Papa seemed fine with leaving the Low Meadows now 'cause he knew she would take care of Ma.

We headed down Stony Hill. Heavy from all the rain, the weeping willows were leaning on Low Meadows Lane. With water still dripping from the leaves the trees appeared to be crying too. The leaves had fallen all over the ground. It felt like everything in the Low Meadows wanted to come alive and walk with us to town to tell Mr. Gordon that the angels came and got Mr. Bro. Wiley.

29

I couldn't keep my eyes off the sky. The clouds were dark again and sad, as if they were crying too. Mr. Bro. Wiley leaving was something to cry about.

"Look like the storm is coming back, Papa."

"Well, I-I sure hope not, but the wind getting high again. White folk in town say a big storm is coming all the way from Jamaica."

"Where's that?"

"I don't know. I send you to school every day when it ain't 'bacco and cotton season. You-you need to look at the globe and tell me."

"I hope the storm don't get here 'fore the sittin' up."

"Now-now, that ain't in the books. Only the Lord knows that," Papa said.

Mule Bennett finally made his way down to Low Meadows Lane. The first person we saw when we got back on Low Meadows Lane was Ma's only brother, Lionel. Everyone called him Goat. He was all dressed up like he was going to church with a nice straw hat that covered his gray hair and slightly hid the patch over the eye he lost in an accident at the sawmill.

My uncle lived down on the riverbank in one of the old slave cabins that he fixed up. He even put a new floor in his house—a tile floor. He got the tile real cheap at the factory he used to work at over in Woodland. He got fired from there just like he did at the sawmill. He claimed he was sick with the flu, but his boss saw him over in Weldon shopping the same day. Now he can only work for Mr. Thomas and I reckon Papa keeps his brother-in-law's lies a secret from his boss.

Ma swears Uncle Goat is the biggest liar in Northampton County. Papa said that ain't so. He said Uncle Goat is the biggest liar in the state of North Carolina. That's how he got the nickname Goat. Ma said he eats the truth up faster than a goat eats grass. One day while we were picking butter beans from the garden that Ma loved so much, I asked her, "Is Uncle Goat as big a liar folks say he is?"

"I'm afraid so, child. I don't know where Goat got his lying from 'cause our daddy and ma were God-fearing folk that never told a lie a day in their lives that I know of. Goat lies to hear himself talk. It's the way he is.

"One day I reckon all my brother's lies gonna catch up with him. One day real soon."

"Well, how do you know when he's lying, Ma?"

"It ain't what he says. It's this crazy look he gets in that one eye the Lord left him with. You want to see him mad, just catch him in a lie. Catch Goat in a lie, and he's ready to fight."

"That ain't right."

"N'all, Son. That ain't right," Ma said. She kept on filling the old rusty bucket up with butter beans.

"I reckon that's why he ain't got a wife?" I said.

Ma wiped the sweat off her forehead with the back of her hand and laughed.

"I reckon that's the main reason. Now get back to work."

"Mornin', Stanbury. Mornin', Bean," Uncle Goat called out when we got close.

"Hey, Uncle Goat."

"Mornin', Goat. You need a ride?" Papa asked. I knew he was wondering why Uncle Goat wasn't in the field working.

"I'll walk. I'm gonna go to Jackson to see my gal."

Papa slowed Mule Bennett down so he could get a good look at my lying uncle.

"Jackson? Gal? What gal?" I thought to myself. He supposed to be working.

"Fine, but-but stop by and see your-your sister when you come back. Mr. Bro. Wiley died last night and Wife tore all to pieces."

Uncle Goat threw his arms in the air.

"Lord, I didn't know. I'll go to the house to see about Baby Sister when I get back." Uncle Goat should have been ashamed of himself. He probably went to the fields and when he didn't see Papa, he went home, changed clothes, and started walking to Jackson. He'd done that kinda mess before. Soon as Papa turned his back, folk in the Low Meadows started doing as they pleased. Even kinfolk. Uncle Goat didn't much like the fact Papa was in charge of the colored folk in the Low Meadows. Mr. Thomas paid Papa twenty whole dollars a week to make sure everybody worked. He paid Papa an extra five dollars a month to make sure all the farm equipment in the Low Meadows was fixed. One day when Mr. Bro. Wiley was sitting on our front porch with me and Uncle Goat eating peanuts, Uncle Goat started talking evil about my papa. I'm not old enough to speak my mind, but it sure made me mad enough to spit.

"Stanbury make me sick. He always bossing Low Meadows folk around. He act like it's still slavery time and he the overseer," Uncle Goat said.

Mr. Bro. Wiley 'bacco almost fell out his mouth.

"Shut up, Goat, with your lying self. You were born free. You don't know nothin' 'bout slavery. Stanbury ain't no overseer 'cause slavery is over. That man is taking care of his family. Now shut your lying mouth." Then Mr. Bro. Wiley took his walking stick and pushed Uncle Goat in the back. He almost knocked him off the stoop.

"Go home, boy," Mr. Bro. Wiley said.

Uncle Goat got up and walked away 'cause he knew he was wrong. He knew better than to talk back to Mr. Bro. Wiley. Nobody talked sassy to Mr. Bro. Wiley, no matter how old they were. Uncle Goat got the crazy look with wide eye and his nose turned up as me and Papa left him standing on the side of the road.

"Get 'em up, Ole Bennett," Papa shouted. I turned around and waved bye to Uncle Goat.

Uncle Goat loved Mr. Bro. Wiley too, even if the ole slave man did call him a liar to his face. He loved him the way we all did. Mr. Bro. Wiley would be fussing at Uncle Goat one minute and they would be playing checkers the next minute. The men would play all night if Ma didn't start carrying on for Mr. Bro. Wiley to go to bed. They did more talking than playing checkers though. They talked about fishing, white folk, and women.

"Papa, are you mad that Uncle Goat ain't in the field this morning?"

"No-no, I ain't. Every man got to answer to God, not to Stanbury Jones. Mr. Bro. Wiley taught me years ago how to handle the folk that live in the Low Meadows. 'Don't let these folks run you crazy, Stanbury,' he would say. 'Tell them what they need to do and you go on with your day. You need to guide them, not stand over them like it's still slavery time. If Thomas Wiley don't agree with the way colored folk doing things, let him come back here and fire them himself.'"

Papa listened to Mr. Bro. Wiley 'cause he said the ole slave man had more sense than every man in the Low Meadows put together. He understood people and how they thought about things.

Mr. Bro. Wiley taught us all something about this world and the folk that lived in it. Now the time had come for us to live without him.

Four

Mule Bennett was moving so slow that it took us one level hour to get into town. It usually takes forty minutes according to the gold pocket watch Mr. Bro. Wiley gave me. Out of all the folks in the Low Meadows, he chose to give his watch to me last Christmas.

"Oh, Mr. Bro. Wiley, I can't keep your watch," I'd said when I opened the cigar box that he had wrapped in newspaper and tied with string.

"Keep it, child. I can't stay on this earth forever. I want you to have it to remember me by," he said. It was as if he saw death standing right beside the Christmas tree that was decorated with strung popcorn.

"I don't need nothing to remember you, Mr. Bro.

Wiley. I could never forget you," I told him. Then I gave him my gift—a box of shelled pecans. He loved pecans mixed with hard candy, but his hands were too weak to crack them open.

"I'ze going to have to hide these from myself." He chuckled while trying to chew one with the few teeth he had left.

"I will never forget Mr. Bro. Wiley," I thought as we headed to town. Mule Bennett must have felt the same way. He was slowing down and barely lifted his head. Papa kept saying, "Get-get, get up, mule, get up." But Mule Bennett took his own sweet time.

When we got to the main road running through Rich Square, I reached over and touched Papa's leg.

"Mule Bennett's heart is surely broken, Papa."

"I believe you-you are right, Son. Did I ever tell you the whole story about the mules and Mr. Bro. Wiley?" Papa asked.

"No, sir, but I sho' want to know."

"Well, after-after slavery the law said that every slave owner was supposed to give each family forty acres of land and a mule. Mr. Thomas's folk weren't about to give nobody they land, but they did give Mr. Bro. Wiley's family a mule and the old log cabin. Told them they could stay in the Low Meadows free the rest of their lives. Mr. Thomas's folk been giving Mr. Bro. Wiley a mule about every fifteen years since slavery ended. When one mule died, they'd give him another one.

"Low Meadows folk said it was because Mr. Bro. Wiley's mama birthed most all the white babies and even gave them milk from her own bosom."

"Ain't fifteen years a long time for a mule to live?" I asked.

"It-it is a long time. But mules are different from most farm animals. If you-you work them hard in the field, they'll last about twenty years. If a farmer ain't too hard on they mule, he'll last about thirty years. Since Mr. Bro. Wiley was a blacksmith, he had no reason to work his mules hard.

"Ain't that right, Mule Bennett?" Papa said. He was always talking to that animal like he was a person.

By eight o'clock, we were turning onto Main Street where the Gordons lived. A few colored folk had little houses in town, but not on Main Street. Seems as if it was reserved for "Whites Only." That was until the Creecys and the Gordons came along.

Mr. and Mrs. Spence Creecy lived about half a mile from the Gordons in a pretty white house that sits right beside the school building. He became our principal when his daddy, William Spence Creecy Sr., died in 1932. Mrs. Creecy was the school secretary.

Folk in Rich Square surely thought a lot of the Creecys, I can tell you that. Lord, Mr. Bro. Wiley thought the sun rose and set on Mr. Creecy. He watched him grow into a fine proud educated man just like the rest of his family. Mr. Creecy loved Mr. Bro. Wiley too. He seemed thankful to Mr. Bro. Wiley for teaching him, Mr. Jabo, and Papa how to hunt for coon when they were little boys.

"There are some things that just ain't in the books that Mr. Bro. Wiley got in his head and heart," Mr. Creecy would say at church when they recognized Mr. Bro. Wiley as the oldest man in the county.

The menfolk learned all they could from him on every hunt. After Mr. Bro. Wiley got too old to keep up with the younger men, they would make the journey alone.

Mr. Bro. Wiley would be sitting on the porch waiting for them to get back. Ma always had a pitcher of ice water waiting for the menfolk. The ole slave man said if it hadn't been for Mr. Creecy and Mr. Gordon, colored folk wouldn't have known the moon from the sun when it came to money and education.

"I'm going before the board of education to ask for new books for the colored children come fall," Mr.

Creecy said to Mr. Bro. Wiley the last time he came to the Low Meadows. Mr. Bro. Wiley looked pleased as he carved Ma a cooking spoon out of a piece of bark I'd found down by the river.

"Books, huh? That's good, Spence. That's real good."

I smiled at the thought of Mr. Creecy getting new books for the colored children. When I looked up, I saw Mr. Creecy coming out of the bank. I was shocked to see the white banker, Mrs. Carter, saying good-bye. She and her husband the white undertaker owned the bank and two white funeral houses in Rich Square and Jackson. It was as rare as a bald eagle to see white folk talking to coloreds unless they were bossing us around.

"Thank you for your business," she said loud enough for the whole town to hear. I reckon he and the Gordons were the only colored folks that had enough money to put in a bank. The little money Papa had he hid in a mason jar under the house.

Mr. Creecy was a tall man but not as tall as Mr. Jabo, who was six feet eight inches tall. Mr. Creecy always walked straight and proud.

"Mornin', Mr. Creecy," Papa said as we climbed down from the wagon to give him news of the death.

"Good morning, Mr. Jones. Mornin', Bean."

I loved the way they called each other "Mister" when children were around. Papa said it would teach us to always respect grown folk.

"Shake his hand, child," Papa said to me as if I'd forgotten my manners.

"Mornin', Mr. Creecy. It's nice to see you," I said. I shook his big hand and we smiled at each other.

"Nice to see you too, Bean." Mr. Creecy reached in his pocket and gave me a brand-new nickel. I looked at Papa.

"Is it all right to keep it? It's not my birthday."

"Yes, Bean, you can keep-keep the money."

"Thank you, sir."

"You're welcome, Bean," Mr. Creecy said.

"What you doing in town so early?"

Papa looked his friend in the eyes with great sadness. "Mr. Bro. Wiley is dead and gone. We on our way to get Mr. Gordon."

Mr. Creecy's face, that always looked strong as iron, melted like butter on the potbelly stove. He fought back tears.

"Thank you for letting me know," Mr. Creecy said, touching Papa's shoulder for a second.

Papa was sad all over again.

"Let me get to this breakfast meeting so that I can go home and tell my wife the sad news." Mr. Creecy left in a hurry. I reckon he didn't want me to see him tore all to pieces.

"Men hurt-hurt too, Bean."

"You think the world of Mr. Creecy, don't you, Papa?"

"He's a good man. He's our hope, child."

"Why you always say he our hope?" I asked as we climbed back in the wagon. Papa didn't answer me for a few minutes. He was looking at the sign hanging over the front door at Taylor's Grocery: FOR WHITES ONLY.

Then he pulled my face up by my chin so he could see my eyes.

"One-one day Mr. Creecy gonna make it possible for that sign to come down. That's what I mean when I say he's our hope. He is our hope for an equal life with white folk."

"That will be mighty fine," I said.

"It ain't gonna always be this way."

"I wonder what kind of breakfast meeting Mr. Creecy talking about," I asked Papa.

"He-he going to the café to eat with-with the white folk. That's where he go-go every Saturday morning. He gonna tell them what else we need at the schoolhouse for the children."

"White folk! I didn't know white folk ate with coloreds," I shouted. "Do they listen to him and do what he say?"

"Sure they-they listen. I'll tell you something else," Papa bragged. "I done seen him a-a many Saturday mornings in that restaurant looking white folk dead in the eyes."

I just couldn't believe my ears. I was so proud of Mr. Creecy that I wanted to kiss Papa, but I was too big to be kissing a man, even my daddy.

"I just got to ask you this," I said as I thought about a colored man sitting in the café with the fancy tablecloths.

"You can ask me anything."

"Do Mr. Creecy go in the front door or the back at the café?"

"The front, Son. And one of these days, we all gonna go in the front door."

FIVE

I smiled all the way to Mr. Gordon's fine white house
that he bought from the Carters.

I bet Mr. Bro. Wiley was tickled to death to see Mr.
Gordon buy one of the biggest houses in Rich Square. I
thought about my friend as Papa tied Mule Bennett to
the pecan tree in the colored undertaker's backyard, just
a little ways down the hill. Mule Bennett got real noisy
when Papa tied him up. He didn't like no rope because
he was free to do as he pleased back in the Low Meadows as long as he stayed out of the yard and away from
Ma's flowers.

I could smell Mrs. Gordon's biscuits cooking as we
walked up the small hill. Papa knocked. I saw Mrs.
Gordon through the screen. She hurried down the long
hallway on the hardwood floors that Papa shined once

a month. The Gordons paid him fifteen whole dollars every first Saturday to do the floors and fix anything broken around the house and the funeral home. It wasn't too much work done at their place or the Creecys' that Papa didn't do (when he wasn't working for Mr. Thomas).

"I'll get the door, Miss Margie," Mrs. Gordon said to her housekeeper. The Gordons was the only coloreds in the county with a maid.

I noticed Mrs. Gordon's nails were painted pink when she unlatched the door. Ma never polished her nails. I reckon she worked too hard in the fields and for Miss Remie to take care of her nails. When I become a lawyer I had plans to buy Ma all the nice things Mrs. Gordon had. I would buy her nail polish and fine dresses with matching shoes. I live for the day when I can tell Ma to never prime another piece of 'bacco or wash another load of clothes for white folk.

Just as Mrs. Gordon opened the door, Miss Margie stood up from dusting the tallest dark wood bookshelf I had ever seen. I couldn't believe my eyes. A white woman!

I wanted to die and go on to heaven with Mr. Bro. Wiley. She wasn't high yellow like Ma. She was as white as cotton.

"Papa, Miss Margie is white!"

"Boy, if you don't-don't hush your mouth."

Mrs. Gordon acted as if she didn't hear me.

Papa made me mind my manners, but I could tell he was just as carried away as I was. He ain't worked for the Gordons in a few weeks so he surely didn't know about this white woman.

I couldn't wait to get home to tell Ma. Ain't no way in the world she knew 'cause Ma ain't said a word. I knew good and well Miss Lottie Pearl with her gossiping self didn't know either. If she had, everybody in the Low Meadows would have known. I heard tell Miss Lottie Pearl wanted to work for the Gordons but they didn't hire her. I bet the nickel Mr. Creecy gave me they didn't hire her because she had too much mouth for them dignified folk.

I stopped thinking about her and thought about Mr. Bro. Wiley. I wanted to go home and wake him up from the dead to tell him about the white woman cleaning toilets for colored folk. I could hear his voice so plain in my ears.

"Bean, things ain't gonna always be this way. If you live long enough you will see this world change. You ain't gonna have to live a hard life like I've lived. No sharecropping like Stanbury done all his life. One day whites and coloreds will learn to get along. The world gonna change. You watch and see."

I wished Mr. Bro. Wiley could have lived one more day. I wanted to tell him that I saw the world change.

"Good morning," Mrs. Gordon said.

"Mornin', sorry to-to bother you, Mrs. Gordon," Papa said.

Mrs. Gordon was brown as honey and she wore makeup all the time. She always had on fine clothes like a white woman and she talked like she was from New York City. She was wearing a white dress with blue flowers on it. She even had on a dark blue pattern leather belt to match the flowers. Her clothes were finer than what Ma wore to church on Sunday. I stood there and wondered how many chairs Papa would have to paint to get Ma such a dress.

"Please come in. You're not bothering me at all. What can I do for you and Bean this morning?"

This was my first time going inside; never had a reason to before. The house smelled of lavender and the curtains were blowing in the windows. I had never seen so much dark fine wood furniture in all my years on earth. Everything matched, even the pillows on the couch.

"The storm is lingering on," Mrs. Gordon added.

"Reckon so," Papa said. "I got some bad news, Mrs. Gordon. Mr. Bro. Wiley went-went on to glory this mornin'. We need Mr. Gordon to come and get the body." Papa took off his hat. I pulled my baseball cap off too.

"My Lord," Mrs. Gordon said. She reached inside the big pocket of her dress and pulled out her handkerchief.

"I know Mrs. Jones is about to lose her mind as much as she thought of that man."

"Yes, she-she is, but Wife know-know that God is able."

"That is the truth. I will get Mr. Gordon." As Mrs. Gordon turned away, I realized she even called her husband "Mr. Gordon." Us Low Meadows folk needed to get dignified. It ain't nothing wrong with acting like the town people. Talking the way they talk. Besides I would love to hear Ma calling Papa Mr. Jones, just one time. That would have tickled me to death.

"He was such a nice, nice man," Mrs. Gordon said softly as she walked to the back of the house. "Mr. Gordon, Mr. Stanbury Jones is here. He said Mr. Bro. Wiley passed on last night."

"I heard him, Mrs. Gordon. Thank you." Mr. Gordon was already making his way to the parlor.

As her husband passed her, Mrs. Gordon must have forgotten she was dignified. Next thing I knew she was shouting like Ma and Miss Lottie Pearl.

"My Lord, my Lord!" she cried out.

"Now, Mrs. Gordon, that's not the way to act in front of company," Mr. Gordon said. "You know Mr. Bro. Wiley is in a better place." Then he took out his handkerchief and wiped the tears from her face. She pulled herself together and went down the hallway with Miss Margie holding her head against her shoulder.

Mr. Gordon was fixing his necktie as he walked towards us. Papa told me years ago that Mr. Gordon put on a suit every day of his life; just in case somebody fell dead and he had to pick up a body. He said that was Mr. Gordon's way of showing respect for the dead. His hair had waves as thick as clay dirt and it was shining same as Miss Lottie Pearl's hair did right after she washed it and put it in a bun. Mr. Gordon's big eyebrows were shiny too, and he always had a serious look on his paper-sack brown face.

"Good morning, folks. I was on my way over to the funeral home. Hold on a minute while I call my men so they can help," Mr. Gordon said.

We waited in the parlor while Mr. Gordon called the twins, TJ and LJ. They had been working for Mr. Gordon since they were teenagers.

"Come with me, Mr. Jones. We need to get a temporary casket to bring Mr. Bro. Wiley back to town in."

Around that time Mrs. Gordon walked back into the parlor. She looked at me with her kind eyes.

"Bean, would you like a jelly biscuit while the men finish their business?"

I waited for Papa to answer because he didn't allow me to eat at nobody's house but the Cofields. I was praying Papa would tell me it was all right to join her. I wanted some jelly real bad. There was no money for those kinda sweets in the Low Meadows. We barely had enough money to put sugar in a pitcher of tea on Sunday.

"That-that is mighty nice of you, Mrs. Gordon. Go-go ahead, Bean, and mind your manners."

With joy that Papa said yes, I followed Mrs. Gordon to the kitchen. I thought about the day I asked him if I could eat with our neighbor Grady and his mama, Miss Sue.

"No, child. Ain't you-you talking about the Depression in school? We are poor and other folk got less than we got if they don't have a garden. This ain't no time to be eating at other folk' table."

We had sho' been talking about the Great Depression in school and how the stock market dropped in 1929. My teacher Miss Adams was always telling us that there was no money and no food, but I didn't know it affected colored folk in the Low Meadows too. We had been poor for so long, I couldn't tell no difference.

"We all-all got troubles till the Depression over," Papa said.

From that day to this one I ain't ate a biscuit at nobody's house but Pole's. We shared a garden with the Cofields, so that was Papa's reasoning for letting me eat on Stony Hill. I reckon it was all right to eat at the Gordons' house 'cause they was rich.

As much as I wanted a biscuit, I was still hoping to

see what Mr. Gordon and Papa were doing. I had never been in the nice wood building where Mr. Gordon kept all the caskets. He wasn't just an undertaker. He had his own factory. The twins built the caskets and Mrs. Gordon put the dead folk fabric linings on the inside to make them look good.

The kitchen was pretty with white lace curtains. I wished my ma had a kitchen like the Gordons'. They even had an electric stove and refrigerator. I figured it would take another five years for Papa to get both for Ma.

"Sit down, child. Tell me what time Mr. Bro. Wiley left this world," Mrs. Gordon said.

That's when I knew why I was getting a biscuit. Dignified town folk ain't no different from Low Meadows folk. They gossip too!

"It was before the clock struck midnight," I told Mrs. Gordon. I looked at Miss Margie's white hands as she served the biscuits. Her nails were unpolished, reminding me of Ma's. She had little nicks and scars as if she had picked cotton all her life like colored folk.

I wished I could see her heart. She had a slight smile on her pink lips and her eyes were dark like a woman that cried a lot. I wondered why she was so kind and didn't seem to mind waiting on colored folk. Right then I wished Mr. Bro. Wiley was alive again, so that I could ask him the difference between Miss Margie and Mr.

Taylor, who don't even allow us to walk in the front door of his grocery. Surely he would know.

"Anything else for you and your company?" Miss Margie asked as Mrs. Gordon sat down at the table with me.

"No, that will be all." She pushed the jelly jar closer to my plate. For jelly I would have told her anything she wanted to know. Anything!

"Bean, what were you saying about Mr. Bro. Wiley?" she asked.

"Well, he didn't last long," I said. I dipped my biscuit in the molasses that she placed beside the jelly. "It was thundering and lightnin'. He was breathing real hard. The next thing I knew he was gone to hev'n."

I went back and forth with that biscuit. I swear to God, my heart was hurting every time I mentioned Mr. Bro. Wiley's name. I kept on talking and focused on my food so I wouldn't cry.

Jelly.

Molasses.

Jelly.

Molasses.

"Did he suffer?" Mrs. Gordon asked.

"I don't believe he was hurting or nothing. He hadn't been well since the Fourth of July."

"I know, child. I know," Mrs. Gordon said.

"He just got quiet right after supper. I think he knew

he was leaving us. I reckon he was dying all day." I was hurting some kind of bad for Mr. Bro. Wiley as I told Mrs. Gordon the rest of the story. I just wanted the night before to be a bad dream, but I knew it wasn't. I knew he was lying back there in the Low Meadows, waiting for Mr. Gordon to come for him.

By the time I had eaten my fourth biscuit my belly and heart were both hurting.

I looked out the window at the menfolk.

It scared me to death when Mr. Gordon opened the double doors to the casket factory. I could see caskets stacked on top of one another like 'bacco in the 'bacco barn after we finished priming.

"Bean, how do you know all of this? Were you in the room with Mr. Bro. Wiley when he died?" Mrs. Gordon asked.

"No, ma'am. I was in the hallway. I reckon I was acting just like somebody with no manners. I was listening in and I peeped sometimes to see all that I could see."

I wanted Mrs. Gordon to stop asking questions so I could hear what the menfolk were saying. That way I could go back and tell Pole. But she never broke a row. She asked me a million questions.

Next thing I knew TJ and LJ drove up. I reckon they enjoyed having a telephone. Mr. Gordon put one in the twin brothers' house, because he knew that death might come at any time and he would have to call them. TJ and LJ married twin sisters named Lessie and Bessie. They all lived together and them sisters sho' did some bragging about having a telephone. Miss Lottie Pearl said there was no need for them to brag 'cause they ain't got a soul to call. The only other colored with a telephone are the Creecys. But Lessie and Bessie weren't thinking about Miss Lottie Pearl. They bragged whenever they pleased.

"Time-time to go," Papa yelled to me.

"Thank you for the biscuits," I told Mrs. Gordon. "Bye, Miss Margie," I said.

"See you later, young man," she said as kindly as if I was a white boy.

Mrs. Gordon followed me to the back door and waved at the men.

"Good morning, fellows," she said to the twins.

"Mornin', Mrs. Gordon." TJ and LJ tipped their hats and waved back.

While she was waving, I remembered what Miss Lottie Pearl told us to ask Mrs. Gordon.

"Mrs. Gordon, Papa forgot to tell you that Miss Lottie Pearl would like for you to call up to Chicago to let the white folk know that Mr. Bro. Wiley dead. She want them to get word to Willie as soon as possible."

"You tell Lottie Pearl that I will do it today and for her not to worry."

"Hop in, Bean. We-we riding home with Mr. Gordon. I'll come back for Mule Bennett before the sun goes down," Papa said.

"Okay, Papa, and I told Miss Gordon what to tell Willie's boss." I said it with pride because I remembered. Then I looked at the hearse.

"We riding in the dead folks' car?"

"No, son, in my car," Mr. Gordon said. "The hearse is to bring the body back to town."

I couldn't believe it. I had never been in a new car before. I rode in Mr. Thomas's work truck all the time and Uncle Goat's car even though it broke down once a week. Mr. Gordon held the back door of his Ford for me—and just for a moment, I was a king. I looked at the silver dashboard with the nice radio. I could smell the black leather. I rubbed my hand on the seat. It was soft as butter.

Mr. Gordon winked at Papa. He was grown and he could wink all he pleased, but I was as happy as a tick on a dog.

The rest of the coloreds might be in a Depression but judging from his car I could tell Mr. Gordon wasn't hurting for money. Papa always said folk ain't gonna stop dying, so Mr. Gordon won't run out of money.

TJ and LJ followed us in the hearse. Folk walking and driving on Main Street slowed down for the funeral car out of respect. The colored women downtown shopping for the white folk waved.

Mama's friend and Mrs. Carter's maid, Miss Lillian, yelled out to Papa: "Iz Mr. Bro. Wiley gone?" She had enough smarts to know that was the only reason Papa would be with Mr. Gordon that early in the mornin'.

"He is gone," Papa said without yelling but loud enough for Miss Lillian to hear him. The womenfolk began to weep and the menfolk tipped their hats.

The white folk lowered their heads like they were saying a prayer. If they cared about any one colored from the Low Meadows, I reckon it was Mr. Bro. Wiley.

"Papa, the white folk look sad too."

"They-they sad for sure, child. Mr. Bro. Wiley was a good man. He somehow made people forget the color of his skin with his-his words of wisdom and love."

"I wonder if they love him?"

"I don't know if they loved him, but he had earned their respect."

"Sometimes respect is all a colored man will get in this town, son," Mr. Gordon added before making a sharp left onto Low Meadows Lane.

Papa was watching me in the rearview mirror. He reached in the backseat and patted me on the knee. I cried. Not out loud. I cried inside my heart for the slave man who loved everybody, helped everybody, and taught us all something.

Mr. Bro. Wiley always said, "The young are strong, but the old know the way." Who was gonna show us the way now?

Who?

Six

Ma was standing on the front porch when we pulled into the yard. Miss Lottie Pearl was beside her along with half of the Low Meadows folk who sharecropped for Thomas Wiley. All the menfolk were lined up like soldiers on the right side of the door and the women on the left side. Pole stood with the womenfolk. I wondered if Mr. Thomas Wiley was on the way. Surely someone in town told him that death had come for Mr. Bro. Wiley.

Maybe it didn't really matter where Mr. Thomas Wiley was. The people who loved our friend the most were with us. They had known Mr. Bro. Wiley all their lives. People who hadn't lived no place but the Low Meadows stood in sorrow. They knew the land they stood on. Land their slave ancestors worked until their fingers bled.

"We ain't slaves, but sharecropping is still a part of our soul that ain't free," Mr. Bro. Wiley told me and Pole last fall while we were fishing.

"How so?" Pole asked.

"'Cause, child, by the time Thomas Wiley loans folk money, food, and a place to live all year, he still has his boot on their neck."

"Wonder why the Wileys gave you that log cabin and make everybody else pay rent?" Pole asked.

"Guilt, child. I remind them of their evil. I am the last former slave in this county," Mr. Bro. Wiley said.

"You free from all that mess now," I thought to myself as I looked at the Low Meadows folks.

Me, Papa, and Mr. Gordon got out the car and stood for a minute. We just looked at all the love on our porch. Mr. Gordon put on his white gloves and opened the back door to the hearse so that TJ and LJ could pull the casket out. Then Papa, Mr. Jabo, and men from the funeral home walked up the steps carrying the empty brown casket. I headed towards Ma till Papa said, "Stand-stand with the men today, Bean. Stand with the men."

I crossed the porch. Deacon Ward and Miss Katie Lou's boy, Ralph, who was fourteen, held my shoulder when I joined the men. Ralph was only two years and a month older than me, but he always acted like a man. I reckon 'cause he stopped school in the sixth grade and worked in the field. Papa didn't think much of Deacon Ward letting Ralph quit school. He said we would never be so poor that I couldn't get an education.

Pole and Miss Lottie Pearl had their arms wrapped around Ma for support.

The menfolk were in the house about fifteen minutes before we heard them coming back to the porch. Pole opened the door. The Low Meadows menfolk tipped their straw hats as the women began to sing. Miss Katie Lou led the hymn.

"I woke up this morning with my mind straight on Jesus. I woke up this morning with my mind straight on Jesus," they sang.

"I did the best I could for you, Bro. Wiley!" Ma cried. Miss Lottie Pearl held Ma back with both hands to keep her from climbing into the hearse. Ma knew good and well that was no way to carry on in front of that dignified man, but her heart was broken. She didn't seem to care. When Papa and Mr. Jabo finished helping get the casket inside the hearse, Papa came over and held her real tight. The same gust of wind I felt when Mr. Bro. Wiley took his last breath came across me again. I wondered if anyone else felt it. I didn't say a word. Just whispered a good-bye from my heart.

While TJ and LJ closed the doors of the hearse, Mr. Gordon placed a white plastic flower on the door. Ma turned her head. She couldn't stand the sight of "the flower of death."

As soon as Mr. Gordon drove off, Ma fell down on her knees. He was taking away the only daddy she had left on earth. The womenfolk got to shouting all over the porch. The menfolk said, "Amen." Me, Ralph, and Pole ran to the end of the path to watch the hearse head up the road for as long as we could.

"Bye, Mr. Bro. Wiley," Pole said.

"He can't hear us, girl," Ralph told her, like he didn't know she was smarter than both of us put together.

"I don't care that he can't hear anymore. Now tell him good-bye," Pole insisted.

"Bye, Mr. Bro. Wiley," me and Ralph singsonged. We knew better than to argue with Pole.

"Farewell, Mr. Bro. Wiley." I could not believe my ears. It was Mr. Thomas's boy Christian standing at the end of his path. His face was as red as a beet.

"Hey, Mr. Christian," Pole said, with me and Ralph echoing.

"Afternoon," he said. Then he was gone as fast as

he had appeared. I was surprised that he said a word because Mr. Christian never spoke to colored folks except Mr. Bro. Wiley. Folks say he almost drowned down at the river when he was a boy. Mr. Bro. Wiley heard him screaming and grabbed his little prejudice hind part out of the water.

After Mr. Gordon was out of sight, all the menfolk went off to do their Saturday chores—all except Papa. He went in the house to try to mend Ma's broken heart. Ralph went with his papa into town on horseback to get Mule Bennett. There was no need to go back to the field because it was almost noon. The women went home to get their pots going as they talked about who would cook what for the sittin' up that would start after church the next day and last a whole week. Miss Lottie Pearl went inside Mr. Bro. Wiley's room and took the death sheets off the bed. Me and Pole stood in the hallway and watched.

"What in the world we gonna do without him?" she said to Ma as they sat on the bare mattress, while Papa fanned his wife.

"We gonna give Mr. Bro. Wiley the kind of sittin' up he deserves before we take him down to the riverbank."

They cried something awful.

SEVEN

Just like Mr. Bro. Wiley, Saturday passed away. We didn't go to church come Sunday. Papa said it was all right not to go to the Lord's house 'cause Ma was tore up with grief. Instead we sat around the house and collected food from the neighbors for the sittin' up. Miss Lottie Pearl was the first to arrive. You could smell her chicken potpie before she opened the door. Mr. Jabo was carrying a wooden box filled with pies that Pole told me her mama stayed up all night baking. I was some kind of glad to see my friend when she came in with her folks, carrying a pitcher of tea. I wanted to see how she was doing.

She had pulled herself together and managed to smile.

It wasn't long before our neighbor Miss Dora Mae,

who lived across the road, came with some cabbage and white potatoes. Miss Moszella brought cornbread that she left in the skillet too long. The two women were best friends. Neither one had a husband, so they lived together. Both ladies had to be well into their seventies, but Miss Dora Mae could pick more cotton than the average man. Miss Moszella had 400 pounds on her bones, so she could not work in the fields. Mr. Thomas's wife, Miss Lilly, liked her sewing, so they let her live in the Low Meadows just like any field hands.

By three o'clock, you couldn't see the kitchen or dining room tables. We had a mess of sweet potato pies, peach cobbler, lemon pies, and green beans.

"I ain't never seen this much food in all my days," Pole said.

"Me neither, Pole. I wonder when we get to eat."

"I don't know, but I sure am hungry." Then her stomach made a noise like a student rubbing their nails on the chalkboard at school.

Pole was so ladylike that her belly making a noise embarrassed her. She disappeared into the kitchen with the women. I watched over the food and thought about how much folk loved Mr. Bro. Wiley. Even in hard times they were cooking food to help us pay respect to our friend. I wondered how folk would eat the next week.

"If there is a heaven and I know there is, Mr. Bro.

Wiley is surely there," Miss Dora Mae told Miss Rose, who lived over on Bryantown Road.

"Yes, Lord. He is surely in heaven," Miss Pottie agreed. She'd come over riding her black horse bareback like she was straight out of a cowboy movie. That kind of talk went on all evening. When folk weren't talking, they were eating. After the grown folk fixed their plates, me and Pole ate.

In between eating, one of the grown folk would tell a story about Mr. Bro. Wiley.

Miss Pottie was a happy woman, so she told happy stories.

"Y'all remember that time Mr. Bro. Wiley got mad at Goat for lying on Bean. Goat knew good and well he ate the pecans that Mr. Bro. Wiley and Bean picked up from Slave Grave. When Goat kept denying it, the old man just slammed the door in Goat's face. Locked poor Goat out in the rain."

"That ain't so," Goat said, walking in the door, trying to defend himself.

"You lying now, Goat!" Miss Pottie said. The whole room burst out in laughter.

It was nice to hear Low Meadows folk laugh.

When Monday morning came, I had a bellyache. I reckon everybody in the Low Meadows stomach was hurting. I had to drag myself out of bed and get ready to go to the field. I didn't like it one bit that I had to work during the week of death. If I could stay home from the Lord's house, it seemed to me I should have been able to stay out of the 'bacco field. But Papa said that Mr. Thomas wanted all that 'bacco picked and over in Rocky Mount before Labor Day. Papa was his own man but he always did what Mr. Thomas said. His goal was to keep a roof over our heads and to send me to college. As long as Mr. Thomas showed him respect, he said he could work for him all his days on earth.

Even in grief, Papa made sure everybody knew to be at work Monday morning. Everybody except Ma. It was just about time for her to stop working anyway so the baby could come. It was nothing for a Low Meadows woman to work up until the day the baby was born, but I overheard Papa say he was gonna stop that mess and he was gonna start with Ma.

Wanting to stay home with my mama was not the only reason I was hot under the collar. I was upset because it was the first day of school. Mr. Thomas went out to the schoolhouse and told Mr. Creecy that the Low Meadows children would not be coming to school for another three weeks.

According to Papa, Mr. Creecy said, "Not this year,

Thomas. The children can only stay out for a week. That's if you don't want me to report you to the Board of Education up in Jackson."

Mr. Creecy was gonna stop the colored children from staying home from school to work in the fields if it was the last thing he did. I wanted to be a fly on the wall at the café when Mr. Creecy broke that news to the white folk. Just the thought tickled me as I prepared for work.

"Ma, how am I gonna brush my hair if I can't look in the mirror?" I asked for the second time as she walked down the hall. Knowing I couldn't see myself for a whole week didn't make a lick of sense to me. I had been growing some kind of fast over the summer. Pole had been growing too. Heck, I might grow a whole inch before the funeral and I wouldn't even know it. Suppose my suit britches were too short. I started thinking about how I could sneak over to Stony Hill and look at myself in Pole's mirror. Or maybe I could just run down to Ole River and look at my reflection in the water.

"Did you hear my question, Ma?"

"Yes, Bean. You can feel, can't you? Brush your hair and go on in the kitchen and eat your breakfast."

"Yes, ma'am." I followed her into the kitchen, where Papa was sitting at the table having a cup of coffee. I could hardly bear to sit down without seeing Mr. Bro. Wiley across the table from me. I looked at his empty chair.

"Everything gonna be all right," Papa said.

We prayed. Then we ate in silence.

"Time to go, Bean," Papa finally said. I stuffed the last biscuit in my mouth. Ma never said a word and she didn't lift her head when we got up to leave. She just kept blowing into Mr. Bro. Wiley's favorite tin cup to cool off her tea. I kissed Ma and ran outside.

Papa wrapped his arm around Mama's shoulders. "Have a-a good morning, Wife. I'll be home to eat with you at noon. Don't touch the-the stove 'cause we got plenty leftovers from yesterday."

"That be fine, Husband." We left her sitting at the table with her heart in the tin cup.

"Papa, this is the first time I can ever remember going to the field and Mr. Bro. Wiley wasn't home," I said as I climbed in the truck.

"That's the-the truth, child. That-that is the gospel truth." Then Papa turned the radio on. That radio was about as raggedy as the truck. He found the weather channel just as the weatherman started talking about the storm coming at the end of the week. Folk was worried that the river was gonna overrun its banks and we'd have to leave our homes.

"Papa, what we gonna do if the storm comes? How we gonna have the sittin' up?"

"Don't worry-worry about God's work, child. He will make a way. If it rains, people will still come."

My heart felt better after Papa told me not to worry. The two men I trusted the most in the world was Papa and Mr. Bro. Wiley. If he said not to worry, then it was gonna be all right.

He kept his word to Mr. Thomas Wiley too. By 6:00 a.m., everybody was in the field working. I joined the others while Papa parked the truck. Mr. Jabo was on the red tractor, driving real slow, while the field hands walked behind him cutting the 'bacco off the stalk. He drove slowly so we could throw an armful of 'bacco on the wagon hitched to the tractor. I always had more 'bacco under my arm than Pole. That didn't bother Pole one bit because she never had her mind on the fields.

"Stop rushing, Bean. Our pay is the same. A dollar a day no matter how much tobacco we prime. We should be in school anyway," she said with her lips poked out.

"I know, Pole. I know. Don't you worry. Mr. Creecy said we'll be in school next week."

"We sure will. I have no time for the fields."

That's when I noticed her gloves.

"Girl, do your daddy know you got on his gloves again?"

"He sho' do. My hands for surgery, not priming tobacco. Did you know that colored doctors work as close to us as Raleigh?" Pole said with pride and excitement.

"And lawyers!" I said, to let Pole know that I had dreams too.

"That's right! Lawyers too. Stop rushing in this field."

Ralph, who was working on the next row, never said a word. He had long given up on school and being anything other than a field hand. Papa was telling the truth about Deacon Ward letting Ralph stop school to work. That wasn't right at all. Looking around in the field made me sad because most of the sharecroppers had only second- and third-grade educations. This is where they'll work for the rest of their lives.

Papa interrupted my thoughts as he walked into the field.

"Can y'all stop priming for a minute. I want to tell you about the-the plans for Mr. Bro. Wiley. We-we gonna have the sittin' up all week and view the body on Friday night at seven. The funeral at one o'clock on Saturday," Papa said as Mr. Jabo stopped the tractor.

"We will do what we can do to help y'all out," Mr. Jabo told Papa. The rest of the Low Meadows folk echoed him.

"We sure will," Miss Lottie Pearl said. Then something

came over her. She got to shouting, "Thank you for the life of Mr. Bro. Wiley!"

She stomped her feet so hard that mud flew up as high as the 'bacco.

The other women praised the Lord with her. They carried on for 'bout ten minutes.

"All right, Stanbury," she said in between tears, "I'll go help Magnolia clean up and write the obituary."

Eight

I was glad when my pocket watch struck twelve. We usually ate a can of beans and crackers for lunch under the walnut tree. That day we went home.

When we got there, Ma was doing her washing in the silver washtub on the back porch.

"Wife, it's hot out-out here. We got plenty of clean clothes."

"I wanted to see if I could get Mr. Bro. Wiley's shirt a little white for the funeral."

Papa grabbed Ma's wet hand.

"Let it soak awhile. You need to eat."

"Did you tell folk that the funeral gonna be Saturday?" Ma asked.

"Yes, I-I did."

I ate all the neck bones, cabbage, and cornbread that

my belly could hold while Ma and Papa talked about the sittin' up. No one in the Low Meadows was buried without a sittin' up. Ma thought it was a sin for folk not to be able to come to the house to eat, to sit around and talk about the dead.

"Bean, your eyes is bigger than your belly. It ain't gonna be nothing left for company."

Ma's fussing was fine with me. I was full again and it was time to go back to the 'bacco field. Besides, if she was fussing she didn't have time to think about Mr. Bro. Wiley.

She stood in the door and rubbed her big belly as she watched us pull off. Me and Papa went back to the field and worked until six. The womenfolk talked about what they were gonna cook and the menfolk fussed over who should be the pallbearers.

The Cofields came to our house soon as they changed clothes that evening. I was sitting in the kitchen, eating peach pie with Pole, while Ma and Miss Lottie Pearl made the funeral arrangements at the dining room table. Papa and Mr. Jabo went on the back porch to smoke their pipes and decide who was gonna carry the casket. The kitchen was the best spot for me and Pole to listen to everybody.

"Don't know who-who to pick 'cause every man in

the Low Meadows loved Mr. Bro. Wiley. They all feel they got a-a right to carry him to his grave," Papa told Mr. Jabo.

"Ain't that the truth. The best thing to do is let the Masons carry him like we always do. That way the other men wouldn't think you showing favor."

Papa blew smoke out his pipe.

"That is-is the right way," he said. He sounded satisfied that Mr. Jabo had made the decision for him. I didn't know much about the Masons; I just knew they were a group of colored men that had secret meetings once a month. Mr. Bro. Wiley had been the oldest living Mason in the county.

"Pole," Ma yelled. "You almost a teenager now. Do you reckon you can be a flower girl at the funeral?"

"Yes, ma'am. I would be real proud to carry flowers for Mr. Bro. Wiley," Pole said as we rushed in the dining room. Her face lit up and she pushed me in the side for a reaction.

"That's real good, Pole."

"Maybe Ma gonna include me too," I whispered.

We went back in the kitchen to celebrate. I be doggone if Pole wasn't walking different. Walking like she had won a teddy bear at the state fair. Nobody in the Low Meadows was as sassy as Pole, and being a flower girl just turned her up a notch or two. From that moment on, I knew it was gonna be a long week around my best friend.

"Papa said flower girls walk right behind the casket. Are you gonna be scared to walk behind Mr. Bro. Wiley?" I asked Pole.

"Nope, I would never be scared of Mr. Bro. Wiley. Ma has been a flower girl at a lot of funerals, so she'll tell me what to do."

Sassy she might be, but I was some kind of proud of Pole.

I laid my fork down so that she could eat the last piece of pie.

"Thank you, Bean."

After we finished our dessert, Pole and me stayed in the kitchen. Papa and Mr. Jabo went for a walk while the womenfolk talked about what songs would be heard at the funeral.

It wasn't long before there was a knock at the front door.

"Answer the door, children," Ma yelled.

I just couldn't believe my eyes as I got closer. It was Miss Remie all dressed up in a navy blue suit with matching shoes and bag. Her silver hair was pulled back in a bun and her nose was turned up like our clean front porch did not smell good. Her blue eyes were not kind like Miss Margie's were. I wanted to take a piece of funeral fabric and wipe some of that makeup off her mean-looking face. She was holding a pretty chocolate cake in a glass-cover plate.

"Young man, is your mother home?" she asked.

I was speechless, so Pole answered for me. In all the years Mama had worked for her, she had never stepped foot in our house. Never!

"Miss Magnolia and my mama here, Miss Remie. I'll get them."

Before Pole could get the womenfolk, they were standing behind us.

"Evening, Miss Remie," they said.

"Would you like to come in?" Ma asked.

"No, I just wanted to let you know how sorry I am about Mr. Bro. Wiley."

Miss Remie had no intentions of coming in because her colored driver, Mr. Jack Faison, never even turned the car off.

"Well, thank you. I feel some kinda bad that I can't come to work this week. You know we were all the family Mr. Bro. Wiley had, so the sittin' up is here. Folk been in and out the house since Saturday."

"Magnolia, you come back when you can. You have ironed enough clothes for me to wear for a year."

"Yes, ma'am. I didn't want you to think I had lost my mind," Ma said as we all joined Miss Remie on the porch.

"Now, why would I think that? Death is a horrible thing, even for coloreds. Take all the time you need."

I could hardly hold my tongue when she said "even for coloreds." Didn't she know that colored folk have hearts too?

"'Even for coloreds,'" Miss Lottie Pearl shouted out. Pole got her sassy ways from her mama for sure. Ma pushed Miss Lottie Pearl in the side with her elbow so she would shut up. I wanted to push her in the other side so she would keep talking. Miss Remie's eyes got big like she had never heard a colored person talk smart to her before.

"I brought you a cake that I purchased from Mr. Taylor's grocery just this morning. You can keep the cake plate," Miss Remie said as she turned her back to us.

"Open the door, Jack," Miss Remie said to Mr. Jack Faison. She should be shame of herself calling her eighty-year-old colored driver by his first name.

"Afternoon, ladies," Mr. Faison said as he got out of the car.

"I'll see you next week," Miss Remie told Ma.

"I thought you said she could take all the time she needed," Miss Lottie Pearl said as Miss Remie walked faster. That's the reason she could only work in the field. She would run her mouth at every house she tried to work in. They would send her home on the first day.

"Lottie Pearl, stop your mess in front of company," Ma said.

Miss Lottie Pearl kept on talking.

"And I know you don't want your cake plate because colored folks going to eat from it."

"I'll be back for the sittin' up," Mr. Faison managed to say before he drove off with his mad boss.

When they were gone, Ma turned to Miss Lottie Pearl, her hands on her hips.

"Woman, you know good and well I need my job when the sittin' up is over. What is wrong with you?"

"Girl, Miss Remie ain't gonna fire you 'cause ain't nobody gonna put up with her ways." Then she grabbed the cake from Ma, went back in the house, and headed down the hall.

"Bye, Miss Remie!" we shouted as Ma ran in the house behind Miss Lottie Pearl. We followed them.

"Magnolia, did you hear her calling Mr. Faison by his first name. She ain't got no respect. That man too old for her to call him by his first name," Miss Lottie Pearl said.

"Never mind that! Where you going with the cake?" Ma asked as we followed the grown folks.

"To feed the chickens, honey."

Out the back door she went. Me and Pole ran outside and looked on in horror.

"Lottie Pearl, you best not throw that cake aw—" Before Ma could finish her sentence, the chickens were having dessert.

"Sister, that ain't the way to act in front of the children."

"Tell them to close their eyes," Miss Lottie Pearl shouted. She was still holding the cake plate in her hand and spreading the cake out on the ground with her foot.

"There! Even coloreds know how to serve a chicken." Then she dropped the cake plate and the top on the ground.

"Pole, fill the top up with water. The chickens need a drink."

Pole went on the back porch and started pumping a jug of water.

"I'll help you," I said, following Pole.

Ma was so mad at Miss Lottie Pearl that she threw her hands up in the air and went in the house.

Miss Lottie Pearl screamed with laughter. Then she stopped her mess and fixed her eyes on me and Pole as we filled the cake plate top with water.

"Children, my way is not always right, but don't let nobody tell you that you ain't as good as the next person. White folk think we don't even have the right to grieve our dead."

NINE

As soon as we knocked off work Tuesday the sittin' up started. The Cofields were the first to arrive again. Miss Lottie Pearl was still carrying on about Miss Remie acting ugly the day before. Truth be told, folk welcomed Miss Lottie Pearl's laughter in our house that was filled with grief.

"I just want to see Miss Remie again. I am gonna tell her off some more," Miss Lottie Pearl boasted. Around nine Mr. Jabo finally got tired of his wife's mouth, so he saved the whole neighborhood from one more story.

"Well, Lottie Pearl, you know you left them butter beans soaking. Let's head on home." Off they went with Pole laughing at how Mr. Jabo tricked his wife away from the sittin' up.

Wednesday was a sad day for us. Before leaving for the 'bacco field, Papa started going through Mr. Bro. Wiley's clothes to take to Mr. Gordon. He laid out Mr. Bro. Wiley's black suit along with his shoes and socks on his bed. Ma placed his shirt that she had washed until it was as white as snow 'side his other belongings.

"Where we going, Papa?" I asked when he turned towards Ole River instead of heading home after work.

"To-to Mr. Bro. Wiley's house."

That was my first visit to the river since death had come.

The truck brakes made a loud noise when Papa stopped, but not loud enough to cover the sound of his crying. I had never wanted to scream so bad before in my life.

"Why did we come here?" I asked.

"Need to-to get his Mason pin. Mr. Bro. Wiley brought his clothes to our house, but he left his pin down here with all of the things he-he loved so much. I got to knock off work early tomorrow to take his stuff to Mr. Gordon."

I knew better than to ask Papa anything about the Mason organization that he and half the coloreds in town belonged to.

When we got inside, Papa started searching the house. There really wasn't a lot to see in the two rooms that smelled like mothballs. Just a kitchen and the bedroom where Mr. Bro. Wiley said he was born in.

I sat on the wooden bed next to the milk crate where Mr. Bro. Wiley had placed a picture and a lantern. The house was not strange to Papa because the Masons had meetings there all the time.

"That-that is Mr. Bro. Wiley's mama. He told me Mr. Thomas gave him that picture. He found it when he was packing up to leave the Low Meadows."

It was hard to believe that I was holding a picture of the woman that brought Mr. Bro. Wiley into the world. I touched her face. She was dark and pretty. Her head was wrapped in a rag and there was no smile on her face, just sadness. She just had to be good and kind to be Mr. Bro. Wiley's mama. In my heart I knew he came from a good woman for sure. While I was looking at the picture, I noticed a piece of paper tucked in between the frame and the glass.

"Can I open the back of the picture?"

"Go-go ahead, Son. I don't reckon Mr. Bro. Wiley would have minded at all."

As I opened the back of the picture, his Mason pin fell out.

"That's what I-I need," Papa said as he picked the pin up and placed it in his pocket.

Behind the glass was a list of names with prices next

to each one. I realized quicker than a rooster could crow what I had in my hands. My history teacher, Mr. Pellam, had shown us slave papers in books at school. The numbers were the cost of Mr. Bro. Wiley's family. The price they were bought and sold for.

My eyes scrolled down the list.

There!

"Property of Thomas Wiley Sr. A baby boy named George Lewis Wiley, born July 5, 1840, $500.00," I read as Papa looked over my shoulder. He could barely read but he understood what we were looking at.

"Bean, I want you to keep them papers. Mr. Bro. Wiley would surely want you to have them. Take-take care of them. Let them be a reminder to you of how blessed you are to be born free."

"Thank you, Papa. I believe I will take the picture too. I don't want to leave his ma down here since Mr. Bro. Wiley ain't coming back to visit her."

Putting the picture under my arm, I folded the slave paper and put it carefully in my pocket.

The gust of wind ran across my face again. Papa jumped.

"You felt it, didn't you?" I asked.

"I-I did! Mr. Bro. Wiley done come back to visit us before we put his body in the ground."

"Sure have, Papa. Sure have."

Ten

When our rooster's crow woke me Thursday morning, Ma was standing at my door. "Bean, you ain't going to the 'bacco field today."

"Why, Ma?"

"Me and Lottie Pearl want you and Pole to stay home and pick flowers. Mr. Bro. Wiley's casket need a spray. I want to fill the sittin' up room with roses and daisies."

"I'll be happy to do something special for Mr. Bro. Wiley."

I knew she would let me help sooner than later.

"We gonna take the flowers to town and give them to Ada Bea," Ma added.

She was Ma's second cousin on her daddy's side. Cousin Ada Bea made flowers in a little room behind

Mr. Taylor's grocery store. If she ain't baking cakes for the store, she up half the night making flowers for weddings, funerals, and birthday parties for white folk. We best not tell her that Miss Lottie Pearl fed her cake to the chickens even if Miss Remie did pay for it.

When Cousin Ada Bea heard that Mr. Bro. Wiley was gone, she sent word to Ma to pick a mess of flowers and she would make the prettiest arrangements folk in Rich Square had ever seen. She said when she was done, her husband, Cousin Floyd, would take the arrangement over to Mr. Gordon.

No sooner than I'd eaten breakfast, Pole was standing at the back door waiting for me. She had her face mashed against the screen door.

"Good morning." She was the happiest I'd seen her since Papa told them that Mr. Bro. Wiley was gone. Happier than when she learned she was gonna be a flower girl. I could see her deep dimples clear through the screen.

"Good morning, Pole," we all said.

"I came to get an early start with the flowers."

"Well, we appreciate it, Pole. Would you like some breakfast?" Ma asked.

"Oh no, ma'am. I ate already."

"Can I be excused?" I said.

"Yes, go-go on, Bean."

"What we gonna put the flowers in to keep them fresh?" Pole asked as soon as my feet hit the steps.

"We can use the old washtub," I said. We walked over to the barn to get a better look at the tub. It was just as old as we were.

"This will do just fine," Pole said as I pulled the tub under the pecan tree.

"Let's leave it here under the shade until it's full," my sassy friend instructed me.

At the edge of Ma's garden, we looked at all the flowers. All morning long, we picked roses and all the sneezeweeds we could find around the yard.

"What about the lilies?" Pole said.

"That's a good idea."

"Mr. Bro. Wiley deserves pretty flowers," Pole said.

We walked in the fields. We went up and down Low Meadows Lane. Then we ran up to Stony Hill and picked grady sages and a few of Miss Lottie Pearl's roses.

"Get as many as you want," Pole's mama yelled from the kitchen window. She had stayed home too so she could finish her cooking.

"Bean, I think we should go down to the riverbank to pick some flowers."

Together we walked down to the place that Mr. Bro. Wiley loved the most.

"Give me my roses while I can still smell them," Pole said.

"That is sho' what Mr. Bro. Wiley told us."

Pole's eyes were not smiling as she picked a few roses that were growing at the steps of Mr. Bro. Wiley's house. "I'm gonna miss coming down here."

"We can still come, Pole. Mr. Bro. Wiley would want us to look out for his home place."

"It won't be the same without him with us," Pole said. I took my handkerchief out of my pocket and wiped tears off her face. Then I picked a big red rose and gave it to her.

"For you."

Pole's big brown eyes that seemed to come straight from her daddy's head were bright again. Right then I had a soft spot for Pole that I'd never felt before. I placed roses behind her ear. She was doing some giggling. With our arms filled with flowers, we went home feeling a little better.

"Good job, children," Ma said, watching Pole fill the tub with flowers from every end of the Low Meadows. I was busy bringing water to keep the flowers fresh.

"The menfolk in the field. How we gonna get the flowers to Miss Ada Bea?" Pole asked Ma.

No sooner had the words left Pole's mouth; TJ drove up in one of Mr. Gordon's three trucks.

"Mornin' to y'all," he said, taking off his hat like Mr. Gordon taught him to do in front of womenfolk.

"Mornin', TJ, what can I do for you?"

"Mr. Gordon sent me. He thought he would save Stanbury a trip to town by having me pick up the clothes and the flowers."

"I sho' appreciate you coming. Stanbury 'bout to run himself to death this week."

"You know I don't mind, Miss Magnolia."

Ma seemed to be in deep thought for a minute.

"Bean, you and Pole go to Mr. Bro. Wiley's room and get his things."

Not only did we pick the flowers, but we get to take Mr. Bro. Wiley's clothes to the truck.

"Be careful not to get any dirt on the white shirt," Pole said with her bossy voice.

"Get the shoes too," I said, noticing Papa had placed the Mason pin on the suit jacket.

We rushed outside to finish our duties for Mr. Bro. Wiley. Pole continued to supervise.

"Careful, Bean. No wrinkles," she said as Ma finished her business with TJ.

"How much do I owe you?" Ma asked.

"Miss Magnolia, you don't owe me a dime. I'm happy to do something for Mr. Bro. Wiley." TJ was no different from the rest of us. He had a lot of love in his heart for the slave man. Mr. Bro. Wiley was always fussing at the twins because they loved womenfolk like Uncle Goat. No matter how much he fussed at them they still came by to bring him a little chewing tobacco for Christmas. They would sit with him for hours. TJ lifted the tub as if it didn't have a drop of water in it. His muscles grew inside his shirt. He was a strong man like my papa. Strong in the way I imagined Mr. Bro. Wiley was before Father Time made him feeble.

We stood on each side of Ma as TJ drove away. It seemed that grief tried to come back into her heart.

"Don't be sad, Miss Magnolia. It's not good for your baby," Pole said, like she was already a doctor. That girl done lost her mind mentioning that baby. She knew good and well children don't talk about babies in the Low Meadows until we see the child. Ma was so sad that she didn't even hear Pole talking grown-folk mess.

ELEVEN

On Friday, me and Pole stayed home again. We had instructions from Papa to help clean the house. Of course, Miss Lottie Pearl was right by Ma's side.

"Bean, we working like Governor Hoey coming to visit us from Raleigh or President Roosevelt coming down from Washington, D.C.," Pole said.

"Don't complain, girl. All of this is for Mr. Bro. Wiley."

"I'm not complaining. Mr. Bro. Wiley is the first person who told me my hands are for doctoring not priming 'bacco and cleaning."

While Pole was carrying on, I was thinking about what she said about President Roosevelt.

"That's it. I can do one more thing for my friend," I

thought to myself. I will write the president and tell him that the old slave man was dead. Folk say that the first lady cares about the coloreds. She might read my letter and ask her husband to send a proclamation like they do when important white folk die. It was something inside my heart that made me feel like I should help give Mr. Bro Wiley a good send-off to hev'n.

"Where you going?" Pole shouted as I ran out of the house.

"To the outhouse," I yelled back.

Pole was messing with the big gloves on her hands, so she didn't notice me when I grabbed a piece of notebook paper and pencil from Mama's living room chest.

It sure did stink in the outhouse, but that was the only place I could go on Low Meadows Lane where Pole wouldn't follow me. I just wanted my private time to think about what I wanted to say about Mr. Bro. Wiley to the president. If Pole came she would surely try to tell me what to write. And she could take a pencil and correct every other word. I wanted to say what I wanted to say.

Dear Mr. President Roosevelt,

I know you don't know me, but my name is Stanbury Jones Jr. My papa's name is Stanbury Jones Sr., and my mama is Magnolia Jones.

We are not city folk and you probably never heard of Rich Square, North Carolina, or the Low Meadows. I want to tell you about a former slave man named George Lewis Wiley who is dead and gone now.

He was born in 1840 and he died just six days ago. I know you have to run the country, but can you write it in the important books in Washington that he is dead? Somebody might care one day, like we all care so much here in the Low Meadows.

Another thing I would like to ask is can you send one of them proclamations that you write when something special happens? You see, Mr. Wiley was special. Special to us! Thank you, Mr. President.

> Sincerely yours,
> Stanbury Jones Jr.
> Low Meadows Lane
> Rich Square, North Carolina

I tucked my letter in my pocket. Then I walked to the end of the path and put it in the mailbox with the nickel Mr. Creecy gave me. Stamps were only three cents, but our mailman, Mr. Cox, would leave my change.

I put my pencil in my pocket and walked back in the

house. We cleaned every room except the living room, where Ma was planning to put Mr. Bro. Wiley's body.

"Y'all children, go and clean the dining room. Clean the kitchen. Everywhere except the sittin' up room. That's for us grown folk to do," Miss Lottie Pearl said like she owned our house.

Mr. Gordon would be back by two o'clock with Mr. Bro. Wiley.

The womenfolk finished cleaning the sittin' up room while I swept the kitchen. Pole washed the dishes and sang "Jesus Loves Me" with excitement 'cause she was gonna be a flower girl.

It took a while for Miss Lottie Pearl to notice Pole was wearing Mr. Jabo's gloves again.

"Child, what in the Sam Hill you doing with Jabo's gloves on. I thought I told you to stop doing that. He ain't got but two pair."

"Mama, I don't mind cleaning one bit, but I got to take being a doctor real serious now that I'm getting older. These hands have to be pretty and steady."

Sometimes Miss Lottie Pearl's heart would just melt, mainly for her Pole.

"Child, I'ze so proud of you and your dream. Ma ain't got many dreams left, but I got high hopes for you. Keep them gloves on."

A tear rolled down the face of the woman who could be as mean as a black snake if you crossed her. She wanted something good for her child. "All right now, we got work to do," she said as we went back to clean.

Pole pulled her gloves up tight as possible and walked up beside me on her tiptoe.

"I saw you, Bean," she whispered.

"Saw what, girl?"

"I saw you put something in the mailbox. What was it?"

The girl had eyes in the back of her pretty little head.

"All right, but you got to cross your heart and hope to die not to tell."

"Okay, cross my heart and hope to die," she said. Then she crossed her heart with her finger.

"I wrote President Roosevelt and told him that Mr. Bro. Wiley was dead. I asked him to send one of them proclamations that he mail to white folk."

I thought Pole would laugh at me, but she didn't.

"Boy, do you have the right address?"

"Nope, but it ain't but one president, so I just put President Franklin D. Roosevelt, Washington, D.C."

Pole smiled so bright that the whole house lit up.

"Well now, you smart to be a boy. You gonna be a lawyer for sure. Mr. Bro. Wiley deserves a proclamation," she said.

Pole's eyes got teary again. I swear if we don't bury Mr. Bro. Wiley in a hurry, folks gonna cry themselves to death.

"Okay, don't start that crying now. If you do, I won't tell you my other secret."

"Other secret?"

"Come with me," I said, pulling Pole into my room.

The womenfolk were so busy talking that they didn't notice when we ducked inside my room before Pole could say jackrabbit.

"Look at this." I pulled the slave papers and the picture out of my drawer.

"Jesus, Bean, these look like the papers Mr. Pellam showed us in history class. Are they real?"

"Yes, girl! Look a little closer."

"They real all right," she said as she jumped around like she had ants in her britches. Anything dealing with school excited that smart girl. "Who's this woman?" Pole asked. She stroked the picture as if she could feel the skin.

"That woman is Mr. Bro. Wiley's mama."

Pole kissed Mr. Bro. Wiley's mama's face like they were old friends.

"You know, Bean, Mr. Bro. Wiley loved us so much, but he had his own family a long time ago."

"I know, Pole. I know. Now let's hide this until after the funeral. It might be too much for Ma right now."

Pole took her dust rag and wiped the picture off like it was more valuable than gold.

She tucked it safely in the drawer.

"Our secret is safe for now, Bean. Let's go get ready for the sittin' up."

TWELVE

After the womenfolk were done cleaning, they started polishing the silverware that Ma got from Miss Remie. When Miss Remie turned sixty, she bought brand-new sterling silver and fancy china to match. She decided to give her old dinnerware to Ma. Actually, nothing was free. Ma's boss lady would happily swap her nice belongings for a day's work. If we had enough money for the month, Ma would gladly take the fine things instead of cash. She would only use the fancy silverware on Sundays, and at Thanksgiving and Christmas.

Ma was still polishing when Miss Lottie Pearl announced she was walking over to Stony Hill to get the cabbage and white potatoes. She said the cabbage Miss Dora Mae cooked "sho' ain't good."

There was nothing in the world wrong with that cabbage, but Miss Lottie Pearl wasn't satisfied unless she was outdoing the other womenfolk. She wanted her cabbage to be waiting on the stove just in case Miss Dora Mae came back with more.

"Bring them blue glasses you won at the county fair last fall," Ma yelled as Miss Lottie Pearl walked out the kitchen door.

"You need me to go with you, Mama?" Pole asked, pulling off her gloves for the one hundredth time.

"No, child, stay here and help out."

Me and Pole had wiped everything in the house down, so I went to help Ma with the polishing, while Pole put the last cleaning cloths away. Ma wasn't talking, so I thought it was a good time to ask some questions that me and Pole had been wondering about.

"Why are we bringing Mr. Bro. Wiley back to the Low Meadows? Can't we just go out to the funeral home to have the last sittin' up?"

She stopped shining the big spoon and looked at me as if I'd stolen her fake pearl earrings from her old tin jewelry box.

"Lord, child, ain't I raised you no better than that? It ain't right to let a man lay in that lonely funeral home all week and not bring him home the last night. A man got a right to come home."

I loved Mr. Bro. Wiley too and I surely wanted him to come home one last time even if I didn't exactly understand what Mama had just said. I stopped asking questions and helped her with the silver.

While we were working in silence, Pole went outside and picked the few flowers that were left in the backyard to fill the vases in the house. When she ran out of vases, she used mason jars.

Mama saw the daisies and her sadness went away for a short while.

"Thank you, *Dr. Cofield.*"

"You're most welcome, Mrs. Magnolia Jones," Pole said. My friend already had a way of making folk feel better.

"I would appreciate you two going in the pantry and getting my green Depression plates. I do not have enough china dishes for everyone."

"Ma, why do you call the dishes Miss Remie gave you Depression plates?"

Pole would not hold her tongue.

"Bean, you ain't listening in school. How you gonna be a lawyer if you don't listen?"

She sat down so she could explain.

"These plates were made real cheap for folk to save money till the Depression is over. The folk who make the Quaker Oats oatmeal put a cup or saucer in every container to keep even poor folk buying the brand. You know, Bean, if you can throw a straight horseshoe you can win a Depression glass at the fair. Aaaaand," Pole said real long to get her point across, "the gas station will give you a piece of Depression glass if and only if you buy a whole tank of gas."

Pole went on and on until she was out of breath. Finally, stopping for air, she looked at Ma.

"Miss Magnolia?"

"What is it, Pole?"

"Why do people really have sittin' ups and why do they have to do it every night? And why is the last night so important?" Ma put the last piece of silver back in the wood box.

"I don't know if it's so, but my papa, Melton Sr., told me that folk been having sittin' ups for over one hundred years. He said that a long, long time ago, folk get sick and fall into a deep, deep sleep. Something they call a coma. He said that the family would dress the body and then put them on the bed or in a casket if they had one. According to Papa, they wouldn't bury folk for over a week to make sure they didn't wake up. You see some of these people weren't dead, just sleeping from the illness. Folk would sit with the dead to make sure someone was there if they woke up."

"What would happen if they did bury somebody and they were just in a coma and not dead at all?" Pole asked.

"I hear tell of a few folk been buried alive, so they started burying them with a bell in their hands."

I couldn't hold my tongue another minute.

"A bell! Why they need a bell?"

That's when Miss Lottie Pearl came back with a wood crate full of food.

"Girl, stop scaring them children." But Ma didn't pay her friend no mind; she kept right on talking.

"Papa said they would have a string on the casket that led inside to the person's hand. If the person woke up, they would pull the string so the bell would ring really loud." Pole almost jumped out of her chair when Ma said that. I didn't move.

"You ought to be shame of yourself," Miss Lottie Pearl said. "Anyway, I got to go back to get my glasses. I don't want to send the children 'cause I'll be mad as all get out if they drop one."

"Are they Depression glasses?" I asked Miss Lottie Pearl so that I would sound as smart as Pole.

"Yes, Bean," Pole said as she twisted her body from side to side in her know-it-all position.

"Stop it, Pole." Miss Lottie Pearl tried to save me from another lecture. "They sure are Depression glasses, child. They ain't made of much, but they pretty," she said as she headed back to Stony Hill.

Me and Pole got us a glass of ice tea and went outside to sit on the front porch and rest our bones.

"Ma never did say why they bring the body home the night before the funeral," Pole said.

This was my chance to show her that I was just as smart as she was.

"A man got a right to come home one last time, Pole."

Not even Pole had a comment for that.

So we just sat there drinking our tea before all the ice melted.

Only a few minutes had passed when we heard a car coming down Low Meadows Lane. Pole stood up to get a better look.

"It's Mr. Gordon! Do you want me to get Mr. Stanbury?" Pole called into the house. Ma came to the door.

"Ain't no time for that."

That black hearse was so much longer than it looked sitting at the funeral home. It seemed bigger than when they carried Mr. Bro. Wiley away. The twins had shined the car so bright that the trees were reflected on it.

"They coming, Miss Magnolia. They coming to bring Mr. Bro. Wiley home."

"Yes, they is, child. Yes, they is. It ain't but one thirty." Ma thought for a minute and looked down at herself.

She pulled the red-and-white apron over her head and threw it behind Mr. Bro. Wiley's chair. She rubbed her hair to make sure it was lying flat. "Don't worry, Miss Magnolia. You look real pretty," Pole said. She smoothed the right side of Ma's dress down. Pole could help Ma look pretty, but she couldn't keep her from crying. The tears ran down her face, down her neck, and all the way to her bosom. Pole walked to the end of the porch and yelled towards Stony Hill.

"Hurry up, Mama. Mr. Gordon here with Mr. Bro. Wiley."

"It ain't no need to yell. It ain't no need to rush. Mr. Bro. Wiley gone forever. Ain't no hurry at all. Mr. Gordon just bringing his shell back to us. His soul is already resting." Then Ma stuck her hands out like a stop sign. She bent her knees, stooped down real low, and began to holler.

Don't know why she told us not to yell when she was shouting all over the porch. Pole ran behind Ma, fanning her the best she could.

I peeped down into the back window of the hearse. The wooden casket was covered in the flowers me and Pole picked on Thursday. I felt mighty proud.

Mr. Bro. Wiley appreciated anything you did for him and I knew the flowers made him smile from heaven.

"Good afternoon, Mrs. Jones. Good afternoon, Bean,

Pole," Mr. Gordon said. He was wearing a fine double-breasted black suit and white gloves again.

He looked dignified, but something was missing from his spirit. His serious face was darker. Then I realized that he was not just the undertaker bringing Mr. Bro. Wiley home. He was a broken-hearted man, just like Papa, Mr. Jabo, and Mr. Creecy.

"Afternoon to you, Mr. Gordon," Ma said.

"Afternoon," me and Pole echoed.

"Where is Mr. Jones?"

"Husband's not home. He's in the field getting up 'bacco 'fore the storm comes. He'll be back directly. We were expecting you at two. Lottie Pearl will be back any time now." Ma was talking a mile a minute.

"Do you want us to wait?" Mr. Gordon asked.

"No, bring Mr. Bro. Wiley inside. The Lord is with us. You just come right on in."

Mr. Gordon and his men pulled the casket out of the back of the hearse real slow.

"It ain't fancy 'cause Mr. Bro. Wiley didn't have no bury legion," Pole whispered in my ear.

"Bury legion? What in the world is that?" I whispered back.

"Boy, you know a bury legion—life insurance."

"Well, that don't make no sense. Why don't they just call it life insurance?" I asked.

"I don't know. That's just the way grown folk in the Low Meadows do. They call words whatever they want to."

I knew Pole was telling the truth because even though the folk at church took up a collection at Bible study on Wednesday night to help Ma and Papa pay for the sittin' up, it still wasn't enough. I believe they sent Papa thirty-one dollars and some change by Mr. Jabo. Papa thanked him and went under the house to dig up his mason jar of money while Mr. Jabo waited with a lantern.

I thought about what Mr. Bro. Wiley told Ma about his own funeral. It was an evening last fall right after supper. We were all sitting on the front porch eating pumpkin pie.

"Magnolia, when I leave this here earth, you sell this rocking chair. You'll get enough money for my funeral. I don't need nothing fancy. Just a pine box to carry me home." Mr. Bro. Wiley never took his eyes off Ma as he ate his pie.

"I will do no such thing. I ain't selling your rocking chair. Besides, you already home."

"Home! Child, this ain't my home. My home is in *hev'n*. I'm just a stranger passing through this here ole earth. We all just strangers passing through."

"I hear you, Mr. Bro. Wiley," Ma said.

"All right now. You know white folk love antiques. You'll get a pretty penny for this chair, I can tell you that.

Sell Celie Mae's chair too. We'll have our seat together with the Lord."

"Who you think got money for chairs during this Depression? Just keep on working on getting to hev'n. God will take care of the rest."

"I reckon you 'bout right, Christmas," Mr. Bro. Wiley said with a chuckle.

THIRTEEN

Hold the door, son," Mr. Gordon said as they got closer with the casket. I rushed over as fast as my legs could carry me. Pole fanned Ma with an old newspaper as sweat ran down all of our faces. The newspapers were filled with good news about white folk but they never printed a word about coloreds unless we did something bad. They gave us our own section called "Colored News." Enough space to let others know if we stole or killed. Never mentioned when we got married or when we died. I wondered if the paper would print that Mr. Bro. Wiley was gone. I thought about my letter to President Roosevelt and wondered when it would arrive in Washington.

I was still holding the door when the Holy Ghost went all over Ma.

"Don't cry, Miss Magnolia," Pole said.

"That's right, Ma. Don't cry. You said yourself that Mr. Bro. Wiley's in a better place." But she still cried until she was satisfied. We followed Mr. Bro. Wiley's casket to the sittin' up room.

"Here, Mr. Gordon," Ma said, watching the men carefully place the casket. "Put him here and put the flowers around him." Then she leaned close to the casket. "Welcome home, Mr. Bro. Wiley, welcome back home where you belong."

Mr. Gordon looked some kind of upset as he reached in the pocket of his suit and pulled out his smelling salts, putting the bottle under Ma's nose. "The flowers look nice," LJ said to his twin brother.

Then they went outside and came back with some brown wooden folding chairs and the other arrangements Miss Ada Bea sent.

"I brought extra chairs for your company. Anything else I can do for you?" Mr. Gordon asked as the men placed the chairs around the house. Me and Pole pitched in. Just one more thing we could do for Mr. Bro. Wiley.

"No, Mr. Gordon. You done more than enough."

He talked to Ma for a few minutes as she walked the men to the door.

"We'll be back at eleven thirty tomorrow to pick up

the body." He knew that Ma wanted the funeral to start on time. Not a minute past one o'clock.

Then Mr. Gordon removed his gloves and put his big hands on Ma's shoulders.

"I have buried every colored man, woman, and child that has left Northampton County in the last twenty-five years. This has shaken my very soul, so I know you are hurting. God bless you and your family."

Their eyes came together, not as a customer and an undertaker, but as two people with something in common. Love for the slave man. Nothing else was said. No more words were needed. Mr. Gordon headed back to town and Ma went back inside.

Me and Pole were sitting on the hot porch when we heard Papa's truck coming down Low Meadows Lane.

'Fore I could say a word, Ma came running past us like her dress was on fire. Soon as Papa stopped the truck, she opened the door and wrapped her arms around him.

"Lord, Husband, they brought Mr. Bro. Wiley home."

"Calm-calm down, Wife. It's gonna be-be all right."

Me and Pole followed them inside as he held her tight.

Miss Lottie Pearl came through the back door with her Depression glasses. She put the box on the dining room table and rushed down the hall to the sittin' up room, but she didn't go inside. She stood in the doorway and watched. Me and Pole stood beside her. We knew better than to go a step farther without permission.

"Now-now, Wife, we got to open the casket. I want you to help me see to it that Mr. Bro. Wiley look-look good for the sittin' up."

Ma and Papa opened the casket. I couldn't see the body but it hurt me so bad to know he was lying in that casket. I grabbed Pole's hand and held it real tight. Miss Lottie Pearl cried too and she reached her big arms wide enough to hug me and Pole.

"My Lord, my God," Ma hollered out.

"The-the Lord will make a way," Papa said.

Ma threw her arms out wide like a giant bird and hollered some more. It took Papa a while to calm her down, but he finally did.

"He sho' look good, don't he, Husband?"

"Yes, he-he do, Wife. He really-really do." Papa turned and asked, "You want to-to see him, Lottie Pearl?"

"Lord, naw. I'll wait for Jabo. I want to see Mr. Bro. Wiley with my husband."

Papa didn't ask me and Pole nothing! I guess we weren't gonna see Mr. Bro. Wiley.

Not yet.

They looked at Mr. Bro. Wiley awhile longer, then came in the hallway with us.

Miss Lottie Pearl followed Ma and Papa into the

kitchen, where they sat for about thirty minutes. The women held hands while Papa got them some water. When he went back into the sittin' up room, he pushed all the windows up. Then he checked the screens to make sure no bees could get in the house. Me and Pole stood in the hall and watched till we heard Miss Lottie Pearl coming out of the kitchen as if she was on a mission from God.

"You take care till I get back, Sister. I need to get dressed," she said.

"All right, Lottie Pearl. I'm gonna take a short nap before I get dressed."

"Come on, children." She motioned to me and Pole to come on the front porch.

"Bean, Stanbury going back in the field for a while. When he leaves, you the man of the house, so act like one. Pole, you stay over here till the clock say it's five o'clock, then you come on home to get dressed. Help Sister if she needs you now."

"Yes, Ma, I'll help," Pole said, but Miss Lottie Pearl had already turned her back to us and was halfway down the steps. Then I heard Papa coming down the hallway.

"All right, children. Y'all stay-stay outside. The door to the sittin' up room is gonna stay closed till tonight."

"Closed!" I thought to myself. Papa made me as hot as pee water. He really did. One minute he want me to be a man, the next minute he got me on the porch like a two-year-old. It just wasn't right.

While I was trying to cool off, he just got in the truck and drove away. He left a big cloud of dust for me and Pole to choke on.

"Sho' is hot out here," Pole finally said.

"It's too hot," I answered. Then I got my handkerchief out my pocket and wiped the sweat off her pretty face.

"Thank you," Pole said, smiling at me like she did when I gave her the flower.

She is pretty as a pie when she smiles. One of these days I'll tell her so. One of these days I'm gonna ask her to go to the school dance with me. She ain't no kin to me. She don't have one drop of Jones blood in her veins and I don't have a drop of Cofield blood. It ain't a thang in the world wrong with us going to the school dance together.

Another hour went by and me and Pole was still sitting on the porch sweating.

"I think we need to see Mr. Bro. Wiley right now. He was our friend too," Pole said. "We got just as much right as anybody."

"How we gonna see him with the door closed?"

"Well, if you really want to see him, the windows ain't closed," Pole said, jumping off the porch.

I followed her around the house to the sittin' up room window at the corner of the house.

"We can't see Mr. Bro. Wiley through the curtain," I told Pole.

She stood on her tiptoes with a stick in her hand, pushing the screen up. She moved the dead folk fabric back.

"It worked," she said.

"Not so loud," I whispered. "Ma might hear us."

We looked in the window at Mr. Bro. Wiley's casket across the room under the other window. There he was. He was all dressed up fit to go to church. His black suit looked brand new and his Mason pin stood out the most.

"He sho' don't look dead to me. He even got a smile on his face," Pole finally said.

"He looks dead enough for my eyes," I insisted. "You know Joe Gordon is the best undertaker in the whole world. He can make the dead look alive. He probably could make the people that are alive look dead if he wanted to. You know what Ma said about Mr. Gordon and why he so good at his job?"

"No, what did Miss Magnolia say?"

"Well, she said the man is dignified. She said he is a friend to the friendless and family to those who ain't got nobody. So that makes him real special."

"Friend to the friendless, that's Mr. Gordon," Pole said, sounding just like the deacons in the amen corner at church.

"Okay, now hush up before someone hears us and we get a whupping or worse."

"I can't imagine what's worse than a whupping," Pole said.

"Worse than a whupping? Are you crazy? You know our folk will catch us out here peeping at Mr. Bro. Wiley and not let us go to the final sittin' up tonight. That is worse than any whupping to me."

This is our first time going to a sittin' up and I wasn't letting nobody, not even Pole, mess up the last night for me. We always had to stay at home in the past when a sittin' up was going on; but not this time.

I gave Pole a hug as we stood there looking at Mr. Bro. Wiley. Then I looked up at the big cloud over our heads. A storm surely was on the way. I thought about how Mr. Bro. Wiley used to say his bones would be hurting before every storm. When that happened, Mr. Bro. Wiley would walk down to the river to check the water. When he got back home, he had a full weather report for us.

"Christmas," he'd yell through the screen door, "that river got waves as thick as a log of wood and my knees hurting. A storm is surely on the way."

"Yes, Mr. Bro. Wiley, so stay away from that water. And you best stop taking Bean and Pole down there. All y'all gonna end up in the bottom of Ole River."

"What you talking 'bout? I didn't take Bean and Pole nowhere. Bean is right here with you, and Pole home with her folk."

"Well, you had them down there last week. I saw you," Ma would fuss.

"Bean and Pole young folk. They can run home where it's safe if a storm come. Don't worry about me. I'll go on to glory if Ole River decides to wash me away. Yes, sir. I will just steal away from here."

Ma kept on fussing but Mr. Bro. Wiley got so tickled.

Fourteen

Me and Pole were still peeping in the window at Mr. Bro. Wiley when we heard Papa's truck in the yard. There was no need to run 'cause Papa would have chased us down like runaway slaves and wore our hind parts out. His limp ain't never stopped him from chasing me when he wanted to and the Cofields gave him permission to whip Pole if she stepped out of line one inch.

"I know-know you two not-not disrespecting the dead!"

"No, we just looking at Mr. Bro. Wiley, that's all," Pole answered.

"Let Mr. Bro. Wiley rest-rest in peace. I ain't-ain't gonna tell you again," Papa said to us as he climbed down from the truck.

"That's right. We got to let him rest in peace, so I'm going home right now," Pole said.

"You do that, Pole. You go-go on home and don't come back without your folks."

"Yes, sir," Pole said. Papa was gonna tell on us as soon as he saw her folks. I knew it.

"Bye, Pole," I yelled.

"Bye, Bean. I'll be back."

Papa didn't say a word to Ma about me and Pole peeping in the window. Maybe he didn't want to upset her. She didn't look as sad. That nap did her some good. I started bathing for the sittin' up 'cause I knew our house would be chockablock full soon enough. There had been talk all week 'bout how many folk from Occoneechee Neck and Bone Town were coming over to see Mr. Bro. Wiley. Not to mention all the folk from Rehoboth Road and Bryantown Road. I knew for sure that Cousin Braxton and Cousin Babe were coming with their daughter, Cousin Mer. Cousin Mer had three children, Coy, Barb Jean, and the youngest, Pattie Mae.

Cousin Braxton's grandchildren never missed school because he moved out of the Low Meadows long before they was born. Mr. Bro. Wiley said Cousin Braxton was a smart man like Mr. Creecy and Mr. Gordon without all the degrees. Just common sense in his head.

"That Braxton Jones is a man," Mr. Bro. Wiley told me and Pole.

"Why is that?" Pole asked as she always did when she wanted the long version of what Mr. Bro. Wiley was saying.

"Braxton said, 'No grandchild of mine will miss school to sharecrop. Let the white folk keep their own children home from school,'" Mr. Bro. Wiley confided. "So Braxton purchased him a backhoe and two mules. He started to rent land from white folk and buy his own seed. That way the children didn't have to work for nobody but him."

"Do you think my daddy and Mr. Stanbury smart too?" Pole asked.

"Sho' I do. They ain't as old as Braxton. Life teached him more."

A thousand feelings were in my heart about Cousin Braxton and all the other menfolk that Mr. Bro. Wiley told us about. I felt bad knowing how much they had suffered for us children to have a better life.

Of course Ma interrupted my thoughts.

"Bean, are you taking your bath?" she yelled from the kitchen loud enough to wake the dead. Loud enough to wake Mr. Bro. Wiley.

"I'm bathing, Ma," I said.

I kept on sitting in the silver washtub and thought

about my old friend. I thought about how much I really did love him. He was mighty good to me.

Sometimes on Saturday evening while Pole was sewing with the womenfolk, me and Mr. Bro. Wiley would stay down at Ole River until the sun faded away. We would do us some fishing and talking.

"Hold your pole tight, boy," Mr. Bro. Wiley said the last time we were at the river together. I had a big catfish waiting on the other end of the line.

"I got it, Mr. Bro. Wiley. I got it." Before I could say another word that fish had yanked me halfway in the water.

"You got it, huh?" Mr. Bro. Wiley laughed as I finally pulled our dinner into the grass.

I would never tell Papa, but I liked going fishing with Mr. Bro. Wiley a lot more than I did with him. Mr. Bro. Wiley could catch a tin tub full of fish and Papa could only catch about five. That's all—five.

It wasn't just the fishing that made me want to sit at Ole River. It was the stories Mr. Bro. Wiley used to tell. He told me all about being a slave when he was a little boy. Mr. Bro. Wiley's sad childhood made me appreciate living in the Low Meadows. At least we were free people. We might have been poor, but we were free.

"Bean, I done lived back here all my life. My papa was a blacksmith for Mr. Thomas's papa's pappy. It was his job to shoe all the horses. I helped him many a day and night. I would hold the nails in a tin cup while he put the new shoes on. When we weren't making horseshoes for the Wileys, they would send us into town to work for the other white folk. We could build fences and take care of their horses. They would pay Massa Wiley, but we never saw a dime of that money."

"What happened to your daddy?" I asked Mr. Bro. Wiley.

"I just remember my mammy cried for almost a year when they sold him away to a plantation in Fayetteville, North Carolina. I reckon I was 'bout eight, but I remember real good."

"You mean you never saw him again?"

"Never. Massa Wiley's money got low 'cause he had a bad cotton season that year. My pappy had been their blacksmith for so long that he wasn't much good in the field. They sold him while my mammy was cooking supper at the big house that used to be right over yonder. When she got home, Pappy was gone."

"What happened to your ma?" I asked as I looked at the empty space where the big house once sat.

"She cried herself to death. Her heart broke in half. Yes, sir, my mammy went away from here the next year. I lived with my sisters and brothers till I married Celie Mae."

Mr. Bro. Wiley didn't say nothing for a minute. His old black wrinkled face looked darker than ever.

He stared at Ole River. The waves were big like Mr.

Bro. Wiley said they get before a storm, but no storm was coming. That day the sky was bluer than I had ever seen it. Not one cloud, but the river was moving as if Ole River was talking back to him.

"There are things that don't nobody but me, the Lord, and Ole River know."

Then Mr. Bro. Wiley helped me pull another big fish out of Ole River. He never looked at me. Not one time. He kept his eyes on the water. I reached over and touched him on the knee. I wanted him to know that I was there for him the way Ma said folk supposed to be when they love somebody.

I thought about all the good times we had together as my bathwater got cold. At least I had his mama's picture to hold on to. I had his watch and the slave papers. I would surely take good care of his things.

No sooner had I'd washed under my arms, Mama yelled from the kitchen again, "Bean, drag your water outside and dump it before folk start to come. Don't nobody want to see your nasty bathwater."

"Yes, Ma," I answered. I finished washing up and put on my clothes. Then I drug the bathtub with wheels on it outside. After I dumped the water in the backyard under the pecan tree, I ran in the kitchen for supper.

"Stop that running, Bean," Papa said while loading

his plate with food. We had more food on the table than we've had all year. Mama didn't seem to be looking, so I filled my plate with food too.

"Slow down-down with your eating, boy. You gonna choke to death," Papa said.

"Don't talk like that when you know Mr. Bro. Wiley is dead in the other room. That is downright disrespectful," Ma said to Papa.

"You-you right, Wife."

"Can I be excused now?" I asked, swallowing my last piece of chicken.

"What about dessert?" Ma asked.

"I'll eat dessert later." She reached over and touched my forehead.

"You sick, Bean?"

"I ain't sick at all. I just want to go on the porch and wait for Pole." I looked at Papa. He still hadn't said a word about me and Pole peeping at Mr. Bro. Wiley.

"Go ahead," Ma said.

Truth was I wanted to see who else was gonna bring sweets over. I knew it wasn't right to lie like Uncle Goat. As soon as I thought about him, he came walking through the back door still dressed in his work clothes acting as if he didn't know about the sittin' up.

"Hey, Sister. Hey, Bean. Hey, Bro." He gave Ma a big kiss.

"Hey, Brother."

"I heard tell two hundred folk coming tonight," Uncle Goat said, grabbing a piece of chicken.

"Wash your hands, nasty." Ma pushed her lying brother's hand out of her chicken bowl. "And who in the Sam Hill told you two hundred people coming over here tonight?"

"Yeah, who-who, Goat?" Papa asked.

"Folk in the 'bacco field said so today," Uncle Goat said with his lies in his eyeball.

"Folk like-like who? I worked today and I didn't hear that." Papa was determined to break his brother-in-law from lying. I reckon breaking Uncle Goat from lying was harder than trying to bring Mr. Bro. Wiley back from the dead. There was no need for me to sit in there and listen to them make a fool of him, so I kissed Ma on her fat cheek and headed to the front porch to wait for Pole.

"What about the dishes?" Papa asked.

"Let him go. I can do the dishes faster and I want my kitchen clean 'fore folk start to come," Ma said as I rushed down the hall. But then Ma said, "Bean, stay right where you are. You need to pay your respects to Mr. Bro. Wiley before company come." Papa still didn't tell her I saw Mr. Bro. Wiley earlier through the window.

Papa, Ma, and Uncle Goat and I stood together in the hall. Uncle Goat reached over my shoulder and opened

123

the door. My heart began to hurt. All I could hear as I walked across the floor was the knocking of our shoes.

When I got to the casket, Papa put his hand under my arm to make sure I didn't faint. Ma wrapped her warm body around me and pulled my head close to her big belly. I could feel the baby kicking real hard. Uncle Goat was breathing hard as he stood over me. We stared down at the ole slave man. I looked real hard. He did have a smile on his face just like Pole said.

"You want to touch him?" Papa asked as he rubbed Mr. Bro. Wiley's head.

"Yes, sir, I do." My mouth said yes, but my hands froze. Ma pulled my hand away from my leg and moved it towards my friend. I could hear Mr. Bro. Wiley's voice in my head.

"Don't be scared of dead folk, Bean. The living are the ones you have to watch out for."

I touched him right where I reckon his heart might have been. Ma was holding me so tight that I could feel the life growing inside her move again, but Mr. Bro. Wiley's life was over. I touched his hand. Those old hands were hard and stone-cold.

"Why is he so hard, Ma?"

"Child, that's just Mr. Bro. Wiley's shell. He ain't here at all. Mr. Bro. Wiley's in heaven with the angels." When Ma said that, Uncle Goat got to crying like a little girl.

Then I heard a thump. I turned around and there he was—Uncle Goat had fallen down on his knees just like the womenfolk do on Sunday.

"Bless you, Mr. Bro. Wiley, bless you!" he said over and over. I felt sorry for him because he loved Mr. Bro. Wiley just like I did. Papa helped my uncle up, so I turned around and looked in the casket again to study his face. His skin didn't look so wrinkled. He somehow looked younger and his black suit looked some kind of nice up against the ugly necktie Ma made him out of the dead folk fabric.

I reckon it was Mrs. Gordon who combed his hair straight back from his face with a little part on the left side. She didn't know Mr. Bro. Wiley like we did 'cause he didn't wear no part in his hair.

"You got your comb with you, Bean?" Ma asked. She noticed it too.

"Yes, ma'am. I got it right here." She reached down and touched Mr. Bro. Wiley's head like she was touching a piece of cotton and combed the part away.

"There," she said. "That's our Mr. Bro. Wiley."

"It sho' is, Ma."

I think she laughed for a second, but I couldn't hear 'cause Uncle Goat was still carrying on.

"Ma, why is Uncle Goat carrying on? Does he know Mr. Bro. Wiley didn't think much of him?" I whispered.

"Oh, child, that ain't so. He thought the world of Goat. He just wanted him to stop his lying. He wanted him to be a better man. Now hush 'fore your uncle hear you."

"I don't want to look no more, Ma."

"Okay. You all right?"

"Yes, ma'am. It's sad to see him in that casket."

"Yes, it is, child, but God don't break a heart he will not heal. Mr. Bro. Wiley's truly free now."

I knew what Ma said was right, but it still hurt my heart to know that my friend was gone forever. We turned and walked away from the ole slave man. Uncle Goat was in the hall crying like he had lost his best friend. We all had.

FIFTEEN

I went on the porch and sat in Mr. Bro. Wiley's rocking chair so that I could feel close to his soul. I could hear him singing the way he used to do right after supper.

"*Steal away, Lord. Steal away. I don't have long to stay.*"

"Sing, Mr. Bro. Wiley . . . sing all you want to," Ma would say as she ironed our clothes for the following day. When Mr. Bro. Wiley got tired of singing, he would just hum. Hum till bedtime.

Come morning, Mr. Bro. Wiley and Ma would sing some more while Ma fried us one egg each and some fatback. After our plates were ready, Mr. Bro. Wiley would pray till the cows came home.

"Dear Lord, I know you hear me this morning. I want to thank you for waking us up and starting us along the way. Thank you for waking us up clothed and in our right minds. Thank you for Bean, Magnolia, and Stanbury. Have mercy on the folk back here in the Low Meadows and all over this world. Have mercy, Lord. Thank you for this life and the life after this one. Thank you for this mouthful of food this morning. Amen."

I would never hear Mr. Bro. Wiley pray again.

When I looked up, I saw the Cofields walking down Stony Hill.

"Evening, Bean," Mr. Jabo said.

"Evening, Mr. Jabo. Evening, Miss Lottie Pearl. Hey, Pole."

"Hey, Bean," Miss Lottie Pearl said.

Pole didn't say nothing 'cause she thought Papa was gonna come outside soon and tell on us for peeking at Mr. Bro. Wiley.

Mr. Jabo had on the same black suit he wore every Sunday that God sent, and Miss Lottie Pearl had on an ugly black dress that she made. Poor Pole. Miss Lottie Pearl made her a dress too. It was white and wide at the bottom. It looked as if it had a big balloon under it. Miss Lottie Pearl made a big ugly green ribbon to tie around Pole's little skinny waist. The ribbon seemed to make Pole's body lean to one side.

"Let's go see Mr. Bro. Wiley before the house get full of folk," Mr. Jabo said.

I winked at Pole to let her know we were safe from Papa telling on us.

"Got something in your eye, son?" Mr. Jabo asked.

"No, sir. I believe a fly just went by."

Pole winked back 'cause she knew that's our code when we ain't in trouble. But before Pole could get too happy, Papa came to the screen door.

"Good evening," he said.

"Evening," Miss Lottie Pearl and Mr. Jabo replied.

"Glad you early so-so I wouldn't have to walk over to Stony Hill to tell y'all how no mannered Bean-Bean and Pole was acting earlier today."

"Well, I'll be doggone!" I thought Papa was gonna keep his mouth closed, at least till the sittin' up was over with. Miss Lottie Pearl didn't look happy. I didn't know why he had to tell on us. Why? Why? Why?

It was sad enough on Low Meadows Lane without us getting beat. Papa should've been ashamed of himself. He really should've. Now I was just saying that to myself. I knew better than to say a word out loud to him.

"What did you do, gal?" Miss Lottie Pearl asked.

"Not just her, both-both of them," Papa said. "I gave Bean a good talking to. They were peeping in the window at poor-poor old Mr. Bro. Wiley this afternoon after I told them to sit on the porch. Peeping at-at a dead man like they ain't got no home training. I didn't tell Miss Magnolia, 'cause she-she already tore all to pieces."

Papa looked at me real hard like he forgot we were kinfolk.

"Being upset is one thing, forgetting your manners is another. Bean ain't in-in the clear either. He gonna rake the-the yard tomorrow soon as the funeral over with."

"I am? Well, that was my first time hearing that," I thought.

"I guess they both will have to do extra work next week," Mr. Jabo said.

"Get-get out of that chair, boy. Lottie Pearl might want to sit there after viewing the body," Papa told me as he opened the door for the Cofields. "Y'all come on-on in and take a good look at Mr. Bro. Wiley. Say-say your good-byes in peace. Ain't nobody here yet but Goat." Papa left out the fact that my uncle just finished hollering. Me and Pole followed the grown folk inside.

"Hey, y'all," Uncle Goat said as he rushed past us, wiping his tears away. "I'll see you after I change clothes."

Everybody spoke softly as they walked in the sittin' up room.

"Take your time. Take your time," Mr. Jabo told Miss Lottie Pearl.

"Come with me, child," Miss Lottie Pearl said to Pole as she motioned for her to walk to the casket. "Come view the body like you supposed to, girl. Not through a window like you ain't got no home training."

"Lord, have mercy, Mr. Bro. Wiley gone," Miss Lottie Pearl said. She reached down and rubbed Mr. Bro. Wiley's face as if he could feel her touch. Then she went to fixing his necktie. She knew good and well Ma already had Mr. Bro. Wiley looking the way she wanted him to look, but she wasn't satisfied unless she helped.

Pole strong. She cried a little bit, but not aloud like the womenfolk and Uncle Goat. I stepped up to the casket and held her hand so that Mr. Jabo could tend to his wife.

"Good-bye, Mr. Bro. Wiley. I am going to miss you," Pole said as she pulled one of the flowers out of the arrangement and put it in his hand. That girl just do whatever she want. I was kind of proud though.

Seeing her put that flower in Mr. Bro. Wiley's hand tore her mama all to pieces.

"He looked like he never been sick a day in his life," Miss Lottie Pearl cried out. "He looks asleep. Sleep on, Bro. Wiley, sleep on. I hope you didn't suffer while you were leaving here."

"He didn't suffer at-at all," Papa said.

Next thing we know Ma was shouting again. Right then I knew that Mr. Bro. Wiley's funeral was gonna be a mess and a half tomorrow. According to Uncle Goat, anytime you go to a sittin' up and the folk crying a lot you knew it was gonna be a funeral filled with hollering and carrying on.

It ain't gonna be quiet like Mr. King David Lightfoot's funeral was last year. He lived in an unpainted house that sat right at the foot of Stony Hill. He was one mean man.

Now, folk didn't just get up one morning and start disliking Mr. King David. He gave them plenty of reasons. He was just plain hateful. Never even bothered to say hello to the children. Didn't talk in the fields. Didn't attend church. Nothing. He had only one son, named Bob, if you don't count our neighbor Real Kill. I didn't know if it was so and I better not ask, but folk said Real Kill was really Mr. King David's blood son by some woman with a mustache who came through here with the circus. She stayed long enough to give birth and leave her baby on Miss Penny's doorstep. Miss Penny died years ago and Real Kill raised himself with a little help from the Low Meadows women. Mr. King David never claimed Real Kill, so when he died he was all alone.

After Papa found the body, he called Bob, who lived up North in a place called Baltimore. For someone who hadn't been home in twenty years, the man Ma called Big Shot Bob sho' got to the Low Meadows fast.

Folk said he came to get the bury legion money. I didn't know him and he didn't stay long enough for us to get to know him. I just remember he came to the Low Meadows in his black Chevy, with his fancy clothes and his pretty wife, Miss Marie. She was Mexican and looked liked an angel.

Miss Marie wasn't a tall woman like Miss Lottie Pearl, but she looked tall because of her long legs. On them legs she wore stockings every day. She didn't know Low Meadows women only wore stockings when they were going to church. Miss Marie had dark hair and a mole on the tip of her nose. She barely spoke English, but I didn't need to hear her talk. Just looking at her was good enough for me. I think every man in the Low Meadows went over to the sittin' up just so they could get a good look at her. She smelled of honeysuckle that grew on the edge of the fields come springtime.

Ma and Miss Lottie Pearl left the field early when they got word that Big Shot Bob was gonna bury his daddy without having a sittin' up. They went to that man's house and took over. They talked some junk to him as sho' as you born. Me and Pole weren't there, but Miss Marie managed to get out enough English to tell us what happened. The grown folk wouldn't talk to the pretty lady, so she just talked to us when she saw us sittin' on my porch watching folks go in and out of Mr. King David's house. We weren't about to tell Miss Marie that Low Meadows grown folk don't tell Low Meadows children nothing!

"'No sittin' up!'" Miss Marie told us Ma yelled at the city man. "'You just pay for the funeral with your bury legion money. Us womenfolk will do the rest. But we gonna have a sittin' up. You can't come down here acting like you better than us. You ain't nothing but a Low Meadows boy just like your papa, my husband, and your brother, Real Kill, if you want the truth. Now, go on out to town and give that policy to Mr. Gordon so we can pick out a casket before the sun go down.'"

Then Miss Lottie Pearl jumped in. "We didn't think much of your pappy and don't feel no different about you, but we gonna bury him the way we bury all Low Meadows men." When Big Shot Bob rolled his eyes at the womenfolk, Miss Lottie Pearl got real mad and the rest of the devil came out of her.

"Go on and give Mr. Gordon that policy! Don't try to keep half the money, because I ain't picking no cheap casket." Miss Marie said that Pole's mama was jumping up and down like a rooster with his head cut off.

"By the way, your papa ain't been to church since your ma died twenty years ago, so his one suit too little for that big belly! Buy your daddy a suit. If you ain't careful, you'll need a suit for your own sittin' up," Miss Lottie Pearl added. Big Shot Bob walked out the door steaming mad.

After the womenfolk ran Big Shot Bob to see Mr.

Gordon, they cooked up all the food Mr. King David had left in his pantry.

Me and Pole were eleven at the time, so we missed the funeral, but Miss Marie filled us in. She said that Ma put Real Kill's name on the obituary right beside Big Shot Bob's name. Right after Mr. Creecy said a few words, Miss Lottie Pearl read the obituary out loud at the funeral, but she skipped over Real Kill's name. That made him some kind of mad. Miss Marie said he stood up and starting acting crazy.

"Hush up, Lottie Pearl. Y'all act like you love me, but you don't. What you and Magnolia put my name in the obituary for if you scared to say it out loud? All y'all going to hell."

Then he walked out the church. Big Shot Bob didn't say a word. He didn't care. He had the rest of that bury legion money in his suit pocket.

Papa and Mr. Jabo was still laughing when they got home. Ma didn't laugh because she and Miss Lottie Pearl were too busy walking up and down Low Meadows Lane looking for Real Kill so they could tell him a piece of their mind. Big Shot Bob and Marie went speeding past the two mad women without waving.

No need for Ma to be mad at Real Kill.

No need for Miss Lottie Pearl to be mad neither.

They knew Low Meadows folk wasn't thinking about

Mr. King David dead or alive. Folk said there wasn't one tear shed at the funeral. Not a one. Well, maybe that's if you didn't count the folk that laughed until they cried after Real Kill showed his sinning ways. Nobody really loved Mr. King David; but folk sho' loved our Mr. Bro. Wiley. His sittin' up was proof of that.

Sixteen

No sooner had Miss Lottie Pearl calmed down, Miss Moszella and Miss Dora Mae came in holding each other up the way two old friends in pain and sorrow would do. Poor Miss Moszella, she done got so big that the floor was making noises when they walked across the floor.

"Help me, Jesus!" Miss Moszella yelled. Then she fainted. Two boards popped up, throwing her legs in the air. Her black dress went clean up to her waist. Papa pushed the boards down with his foot, while Miss Dora Mae held her dress before everyone saw her big white cotton bloomers. Ma helped cover Miss Moszella's private parts and Pole was fanning her with an old *Life* magazine that Ma got from Miss Remie.

"Bean, get the smelling salts," Ma said.

I ran in the hall to get the salts out the desk drawer. You would think it was worth a million dollars the way Ma kept it in the pink Depression bottle. She had the glass all wrapped up in dead folk fabric.

I was running back to the sittin' up room when I bumped into Pole. Down went the smelling salts! The bottle landed on the floor and broke into pieces.

"Look what you done, girl!"

"I didn't do it! You did. I was coming to see what was taking you so long."

"So long? I just left the room. Now you done broke Ma's favorite piece of Depression glass."

Ma loved that one piece 'cause Papa gave it to her. He got it when he bought a whole thirty gallons of gas in Jackson for Mr. Thomas's truck. He said Mr. Thomas's wife, Miss Ellen, didn't want no cheap Depression glass. She had fine china like the Gordons and Miss Remie. Papa was glad that the white folk didn't want the Depression glass. It gave him a chance to give Ma a real present.

Ma heard the crash. Next thing I knew she was running down the hallway looking at me like I'd dropped the baby she was carrying in her belly.

"Bean, please tell me you didn't break my Depression glass!"

"No, Ma, I didn't drop it. Pole ran into me and made it fall right out of my hand. I swear she did."

Ma popped me in the back of the head with her hand.

"Stop swearing, boy." Then she looked down at her pretty bottle all broke into pieces.

"I'm real sorry," Pole finally said as she rubbed Ma's arm.

Miss Lottie Pearl came running in the hallway acting as if it was her smelling salts on the floor.

"No need to worry, Sister. I got plenty smelling salts. You children run up to Stony Hill and get it. Pole, you know where it is. Now bring it back without breaking it."

"Yes, ma'am," Pole said, already running out the back door. I was right behind her.

But Ma came to her senses. "Bean, where are you going? Come back in this house and clean this salt up."

"Ma!" I said before I remembered who I was talking to. I didn't have to turn around to know that Ma's hands were on her hips and I was in trouble.

"Boy, don't 'Ma' me. I will take care of you after the sittin' up. Now get in this house before I get you for old and new."

"Yes, ma'am." I never understood what Ma meant by getting me for old and new. Heck, she whips me within five seconds every time I do something wrong.

It didn't take long for Pole to get back from Stony Hill. We stood in the doorway and waited to see how long it would take for Miss Moszella to come back amongst the living. When she fainted at church, she sometimes woke up right away or she took her own sweet time. It depended on if she had a solo to sing. She would jump up quickly if she was on the program to sing. If she wasn't on the program, she would just lie there and take a nap.

"You all right?" Ma asked Miss Moszella as she put the salts under her nose for the third time. Miss Dora Mae was still holding her friend's dress down.

"Yes, child, I'll be fine." The men were glad Miss Moszella was awake so that she could stand up on her own. On the count of three, Papa and Mr. Jabo helped her to her feet. By the time the sun set, our house was full of folk. All was calm in the house but the wind got higher outside. The women went in the kitchen to get supper ready. The menfolk sat around talking about the storm. Me and Pole walked from room to room to make sure we didn't miss a word spoken.

We were making our way to the front porch again when we noticed a car pulling up in the front yard.

"Who in the world is that?" Pole asked.

"Don't know, but they colored." We looked a little closer.

"It's Reverend Hornbuckle!" Pole said as she rushed to the screen door.

Reverend Hornbuckle had gone out and bought himself a brand-new car. I wondered what the deacons would have to say about that. He better watch his spending because four winters ago they got rid of Reverend Luther Reiding for the very same reason. Folk said he got too big for his britches. They also claimed that Reverend Reiding was missing too many Sundays from the pulpit, but that wasn't so. The truth was he was put out of Sandy Branch Church because he dressed too fine for the Low Meadows menfolk and he had a fancy car.

Papa is a deacon and I heard him telling Ma what the other deacons were saying while they were sitting on the back porch courting one Friday night. He didn't have money to take Ma to the picture show, so they had homemade vanilla ice cream and talked for hours.

"I-I got my own family to worry about. I got to keep clothes on Bean's back and your back. Not to mention looking out for Mr. Bro. Wiley. I don't have no time to worry 'bout what-what Reverend Reiding is wearing," Papa said as I listened from the kitchen.

Ma smiled at him as she put a big spoon of ice cream in his mouth.

"That's what I love about you, Husband. You ain't got a jealous bone in your body. You a good man." Then she kissed him right on his lips.

Papa was a righteous man and I believed he felt just the way he said. But the other deacons voted and kicked Reverend Reiding out before he could button another suit. I don't know what came of the preacher. All I know is he packed his mess and left Rich Square for good. The deacons might as well kept Reverend Reiding because Reverend Hornbuckle arrived and he had enough suits for three preachers.

SEVENTEEN

Me and Pole ran outside to say hello to Reverend Hornbuckle. We wanted to get a good look at his new Ford. It wasn't just any old Ford. It was a two-door black coupe.

"Evening, Reverend Hornbuckle," me and Pole said. We tried to stand up straight and look dignified as he sucked in his stomach to get his belly from behind the steering wheel. He was so big that everything he did was a task just like poor Miss Moszella.

"Evening, children. How are you?" he said as he wiped the sweat off his brown skin.

"I'm fine," I said.

"Me too," Pole chimed in.

"Good, good," the reverend said as he stared at the sky. "Look at them dark clouds. That storm is surely heading our way."

"Yes, sir, I believe so, but not before the sittin' up."
I sounded like the weatherman on the radio over in
Jackson.

"Oh, child, the Lord don't wait on us to do our business down here. If he wants it to storm, it will storm."

"You sho' got a nice new car, Reverend Hornbuckle,"
Pole blurted out.

I joined in the praise.

"Yes! You got a mighty fine car."

He rubbed the hood of his Ford like he wasn't used
to having nothing nice. You would never catch Mr. Gordon doing such mess as rubbing his car down. I believe
the reverend had what Mr. Bro. Wiley used to call "new
money."

"A man with new money is a fool," Mr. Bro. Wiley
would say and laugh till he cried.

"Well, thank you, children! I got it last week," Reverend Hornbuckle bragged. He need not to be bragging
'cause he was gonna wish he'd never seen that black
coupe when the deacons got wind of it.

"I thought we were in a Depression," Pole whispered
to me.

"We are," I whispered back.

"Look like to me Reverend Hornbuckle should have
been thinking about how the folk at Sandy Branch Baptist

Church was gonna eat come winter instead of buying a new car," Pole said. Wasn't sure if the preacher heard my sassy friend, but she didn't seem to care. She got a whole lot of Miss Lottie Pearl in her as sho' as Mr. Bro. Wiley was dead in the house.

"Stop bothering the reverend," Ma told us as she came on the porch, but she rolled her eyes when she saw the coupe shining like a brand-new penny.

"Evening to you, Reverend Hornbuckle," Ma said, still eyeing the car.

"Evening to you, Sister Jones. I'm some kinda sorry for your loss."

"Thank you, Reverend. Now come on inside and make yourself comfortable. Those children better mind their manners and stop asking into your business. Besides, I'm sure you want to eat before we have prayer and sing. Can't have a sittin' up on an empty stomach, now, can we?"

"Sister Jones, you know me too well. I've been thinking about this good ole Low Meadows food all day."

"I'm hungry too," Pole whispered.

"Me too," I whispered back, knowing good and well I'd already ate my supper. Me and Pole followed Ma and Reverend Hornbuckle inside. He ought to be ashamed of himself only coming to our house on Friday night. Mr. Bro. Wiley been dead a whole week. He should've come by and prayed with Ma as soon as he got word. The good reverend sho' needed to get to know us Low Meadows folk better than he did.

The devil got a hold of me because I wanted the deacons to see Reverend Hornbuckle's car so bad, I almost screamed "fire," just so everybody would run outside. If I had done that, me and Mr. Bro. Wiley would have been buried the same day, 'cause Ma would have killed me for sure.

"Evening, folks," Reverend Hornbuckle said, taking off his hat.

"Evening," everyone said. Reverend had some nice hats. To add to his collection, Ma's only sister, Juanita, brought him a new hat every time she came home from Harlem. Ma said Aunt Juanita bought Reverend Hornbuckle hats because she said church folk up North always give their preacher a gift. She been buying hats like it ain't even a Depression. Ma can say what she want, Aunt Juanita just as sweet as honey for the reverend. He ain't got no wife and she ain't got no husband. She was married to a white man up North named Sam for a hot minute. Ma said Aunt Juanita met him while she was dancing at the Cotton Club on Lenox Avenue in Harlem.

Aunt Juanita was as pretty as a picture and light enough to dance at the Cotton Club, where white men loved to see high-yellow-colored women, according to Uncle Goat. Ma was some kind of upset with my aunt for becoming a dancer. Uncle Goat said that after the riots, the Cotton Club closed for a while before moving to Broadway Street. While Aunt Juanita was out of work, she married the rich white man.

Sam never bothered to come South to meet us and he told my aunt that his folk said she could never come to Boston. Aunt Juanita grew tired of his rules and divorced him two years after they were married. After the divorce, she came to Low Meadows Lane with a broken heart. She left sweet on Reverend Hornbuckle.

I took Reverend Hornbuckle's hat out of his hand and placed it on the hat stand with Papa's old worn-out hats.

I was getting ready to offer Reverend Hornbuckle a seat when our neighbor Miss Florenza Tann and her daughter, Sara, walked in the front door. Miss Florenza had on red from head to toe. Must have been her favorite color, 'cause she wore red almost every day. She sho' looked good in that red dress up against her light skin and red hair. She and Sara the only colored folk I've ever seen with red hair that wasn't straight. It was as nappy as sheep's wool.

"Don't Miss Florenza know better than to wear red to a sittin' up?" Pole said.

"Reckon not," I answered in between laughs.

"Evening, Reverend. So good to see you," Miss Florenza said.

"Speak to the reverend," Miss Florenza said to Sara, who stood there like the cat had her tongue. The girl still didn't half talk to nobody.

"Hey there, Sara," Pole said.

"Hello, everyone," Sara finally said. She spoke so fine and proper. Then she sat down in the corner by herself. I wondered if it made her sad the way the womenfolk treated Miss Florenza. Truth was Miss Florenza wasn't thinking about what folk said. She was husband hunting. I'm telling you the womenfolk from the Low Meadows to New York City were after the good reverend. They didn't care that he was as big as a washtub, the women knew they would be in high cotton to have a preacher for a husband. Miss Florenza told everybody in the Low Meadows that she was gonna be the next first lady of Sandy Branch Church one day. Ma said that's just wishful thinking on her part. Marrying Miss Florenza would get Reverend Hornbuckle booted out of Sandy Branch Baptist Church quicker than his nice suits or that new car.

"Where you been, Florenza? Mr. Bro. Wiley been dead since last week and you ain't showed your face one time?" Miss Lottie Pearl asked.

Miss Florenza didn't pay Pole's mama no mind.

"Can I fix you a plate?" Miss Florenza asked as if we were having the sittin' up at her house and not ours.

"Well, that would be up to the Jones family," Reverend Hornbuckle said 'cause Ma was giving him the Evil Eye.

"Sure, Florenza. Go right ahead," Ma said. But she and Miss Lottie Pearl were as hot as a Coke sitting in the sunshine. I'm telling you, them womenfolk were madder than a wet hen.

The Low Meadows women been mad at Miss Florenza from day one. She was just too fancy for them in her high heels and dresses above her knees. On top of that she sold more liquor than any bootlegger in the country.

Then she moved in the house right next to Uncle Goat and nobody really knew where she came from. She claimed she was half white and kin to Mr. Thomas. If she kin to Mr. Thomas, she sho' didn't look like it with that nappy hair.

All I know is things ain't been the same on Low Meadows Lane since Miss Florenza and Sara arrived that hot Saturday two summers ago. It was midday and I was up on Stony Hill playing One-Two-Three Red Light with Pole.

"Look, Pole, a taxicab coming."

"It's a taxicab all right! Can't be your aunt Juanita 'cause she ain't due back till Christmas!" Pole said.

"Nope, and it ain't Willie. 'Cause you know Papa and Mr. Jabo pick him up from the train station."

When the taxicab stopped and the dust settled, Miss Florenza got out of the car like she was the queen of England. Her lips were all covered in red lipstick and her hair was red. Her face was filled with rouge and eye shadow. She was surely not from these parts.

"Well, hello, children. I'm Florenza. Florenza Tann."

"Hello, Miss Florenza," Pole said. "My name is Martha Rose. Folk here in the Low Meadows call me Pole. This is Stanbury Jr. Folk call him Bean."

I peeped inside the cab and laid eyes on Sara for the first time. She was crying to beat the band.

"Why you crying?" Pole asked.

"That's Sara and she crying because she doesn't want to live in the South." Miss Florenza said it as if crying was routine for the little redhead.

Pole waved at Sara. The city girl looked at Pole and cried louder.

"Don't be offended. She just has to get used to her new neighbors."

"Neighbors? You mean you're moving to the Low Meadows?" Pole asked all excited.

"Yes, I'm looking for Christian Wiley's house. His daddy told me to see him as soon as we arrived. We gonna be renting the little house down at the river. He left the key with his son."

Before we could answer Miss Florenza, Miss Lottie Pearl was standing on the edge of Stony Hill with her neck stuck out like a peacock.

"His house is the third one on the left," she said in her not-so-nice voice. Then she looked at our soon-to-be neighbor's shoes. "Red shoes. A sinner for sure," Miss Lottie Pearl said loud enough for everyone to hear.

Miss Florenza went on about her business with Sara screaming in the backseat. Me and Pole ran behind the car. Miss Lottie Pearl didn't even know we were gone because she went running to tell Ma about the stranger moving in. Mr. Christian gave Miss Florenza the key, and she went to her new home. Me and Pole watched the whole thing. I'm telling you, it was a mess in the Low Meadows that weekend as Miss Florenza threw herself a party that night. Some of the single menfolk went to dance and buy liquor that she must have brought in her suitcase. The womenfolk just could not believe it. They did not drink liquor, so they surely could not understand a woman selling it.

On Sunday morning Miss Florenza caught a ride to church with Uncle Goat. She had on another red dress. Sara was dressed in white from head to toe. The Low Meadows womenfolk were so mad they couldn't wait for church to let out as they whispered about her party the night before. It was time for them to teach our new neighbor some manners. They kept on their best dresses. They tucked their Bibles under their arms and walked down to Miss Florenza's house like a herd of cows. Mr. Bro. Wiley tried to stop them, but they wouldn't listen. "Y'all need to mind your business. That woman don't have to answer to nobody but God." I knew it was gonna be a bad day when they ignored Mr. Bro. Wiley. They just kept on walking so fast that dust was flying up higher than Mule Bennett could kick.

Miss Florenza must've got word they was coming 'cause she was sitting on the porch still in her red dress, waiting with fire in her eyes. To add to her attire, she had pulled up one of Miss Lottie Pearl's big red roses and stuck it behind her ear. There she was sitting in the sunshine. Me and Pole watched from Stony Hill. Ralph saw the action rising and he came to join us.

"This gonna be a mess as sho' as you born," Ralph said as he sat down next to us on the top of the hill.

"It sho' is," I added. Pole looked down at her ma leading the womenfolk.

Lord, they fussed. They read the Bible to the sinner. They prayed. Miss Florenza just laughed and fanned herself with her red fan while Sara watched from the window. Uncle Goat went home and peeped out his window too. He knew he was in trouble for giving the sinner a ride to church.

"Bless her, Lord, 'cause she know not what she do," Miss Dora Mae prayed.

"Have mercy on her, God," Ma continued.

Next thing I knew Miss Lottie Pearl ran on the porch to lay hands on the sinner for healing.

"Oh no, you don't, crazy woman! You can praise God all you want, but don't touch me," Miss Florenza shouted.

As the womenfolk pulled Miss Lottie Pearl off the porch, Miss Florenza reached her hand in the window and turned her radio on. You could hear the juke joint music all over the Low Meadows. Music that she continued to play every night while she sells liquor to anyone with fifty cents to spare.

Miss Lottie Pearl grabbed the rose out of the sinner's hair on the way down the steps. Then she told her off real good as the womenfolk dragged her away kicking and screaming. She called Miss Florenza everything except a child of God.

"And stop stealing my roses!" Miss Lottie Pearl managed to get out before she called her "no good" one last time.

"Go on home. You ole fool!" Miss Florenza yelled

back. Then she turned the radio up louder and danced around on the porch like I reckon Aunt Juanita did at the Cotton Club. Sara disappeared from the window. Uncle Goat did too.

Eighteen

It seemed the Low Meadows women never recovered from the pretty woman with the short dress and a pantry filled with liquor. This sittin' up would be no different. Those same women had their mouths poked out now. Just the sight of poor Miss Florenza could start some mess. Now, on the other hand, the menfolk were looking at Miss Florenza like she was a piece of red velvet cake. I think the menfolk tried not to peep, but they just couldn't help themselves. It was something about her that was more beautiful than Miss Marie. I think it had something to do with her sinning ways.

When TJ came in the door to bring a pie that Lessie sent, he looked at Miss Florenza like he was under a spell. Then he followed her to the kitchen while she got the reverend a plate.

"Come on, Bean. Let's go and see what's going on," Pole said, already headed to the kitchen.

"Can you fix me a plate?" TJ asked Miss Florenza.

"Where's your wife?" Ma asked, rushing in.

"Bessie and Lessie at the funeral home helping Mrs. Gordon fold the obituaries for tomorrow."

"That's all well and good. Then go pick your wife and sister-in-law up. Surely they need a ride home." While Ma was giving TJ a tongue-lashing, Miss Florenza took the reverend his plate. He was waiting for her in the dining room. Ma didn't say a word to me and Pole. She just gave us the "go somewhere and sit down" look. Next thing I knew, a loud scream came from the sittin' up room.

"I believe that's Miss Katie Mae," Pole said.

"Lord, I know I been changed," she cried out. "The angels in hev'n done changed my name."

We ran right past Sara, who had not moved from her chair since she walked in the door.

"I bet you a quarter she shouts louder than Miss Moszella," Pole said with a laugh. She knew good and well she didn't have no quarter. We grabbed us a chair. We wanted to get a good look. Miss Katie Mae was really upset about Mr. Bro. Wiley. When Mr. Bro. Wiley took sick, she would always come by the house and say a prayer with him since she was the deacon's wife and the head steward at our church. She would fix him a plate of her good cooking and listen to the radio with him.

"It's all right, honey. It's all right," Deacon Ward told his wife. Ralph looked real upset as he watched his mama carrying on.

"Where's the body? I want to see Mr. Bro. Wiley one last time. Where is he?" Miss Katie Mae asked.

"Right here, honey, but you got to open your eyes to see him," Deacon Ward said.

"This is our last prayer, Mr. Bro. Wiley. This is our last prayer," Miss Katie Mae said as she and Deacon Ward viewed the body. Ralph looked at Mr. Bro. Wiley too but he showed no emotion. He loved the slave man but Ralph ain't never cried as long as I known him. While they were carrying on, Real Kill arrived. He looked drunk and crazy as a bedbug.

"Hey, Pretty Flo," Real Kill said to Miss Florenza as she came in to see who was doing all that crying.

"I said, *hey,* Pretty Florenza."

The woman acted like he wasn't even there.

Papa didn't take too kindly to folk being disrespectful in his house. He didn't drink, so there was no drinking allowed in our house. Ma knew it was 'bout to be a mess if Real Kill didn't hush his mouth.

"Sweet, sweet Florenza . . . I love you, gal," Real

Kill said. Then he wrapped his arms around his skinny body that looked liked Mr. King David's use to look. He danced slowly in the middle of the floor like he was in love.

"Real Kill, this-this is a sittin' up for Mr. Bro. Wiley. You ain't gonna be-be carrying on in my house. You need to-to leave," Papa said.

"Hush your mouth, man. I ain't going nowhere without Miss Florenza," Real Kill said.

"All right, Real Kill, I'm warn-warning you-you to get on out of here with-with your-your mess now."

"I said, hush up, Stanbury, with your *no-no* talking self," Real Kill said with a big laugh. I couldn't talk back to a grown-up but I didn't particularly like Real Kill making fun of my papa. I had to remember what Mr. Bro. Wiley told me and Pole: "Don't worry about what folk call you. Just worry about what you answer to."

Mr. Bro. Wiley must have forgot to tell Papa what he told me because Papa was madder than all get out. His face was twisted with anger as he sized Real Kill up for a whupping.

Right then Uncle Goat walked in the door just as clean as a ten-penny nail. He had on a nice green suit like Reverend Hornbuckle's brown suit. My uncle had no children and no wife, so he spent his money on clothes and women. I was wondering what took him so long till he took his hat off. His hair was usually nappy but now it was as straight as Mr. Thomas's hair. He had gone home and put enough cooking grease in his hair to fry a chicken. Poor Uncle Goat's chest was out with foolish pride of what he thought of himself without anyone telling him. Ma just shook her head at her brother.

But I was glad to see Uncle Goat, because he was good friends with Real Kill. Maybe he could make him shut his mouth.

"Real Kill, you best leave Stanbury be. He ain't playing with you," Uncle Goat said.

Too late!

Papa took a deep breath like he was gathering enough wind to blow the house down. He didn't even bother to open the screen door that he'd made himself last winter. Papa picked Real Kill up and threw him out the door, over the porch railing, and onto the ground.

Bam!

Down he went!

When Real Kill landed, the screen door was under him like a bed. He opened his eyes and stared straight at the sky. He looked at me and Pole standing on the porch and he glanced at Mr. and Mrs. Creecy, who had parked their car alongside the road and just walked up to the house. Ma was some kind of embarrassed in front of the dignified town folk. Mr. Creecy was dressed fine and he had clearly just left the barbershop with such a nice haircut. Mrs. Creecy had on black from head to toe. It made her gray hair look almost blue against her paper-sack brown skin. The dignified folk weren't used to this kinda carrying on, but Ralph was loving every minute of it. He wasn't so smart, but he was a good boxer. That boy would sit by the radio for hours listening to reruns of Joe Louis's 1938 rematch against fighter Max Schmeling. At that moment, I realized he had dreams too. Ralph wanted to be a prizefighter one day. That night he had a ringside seat.

"Lord, have mercy, Husband!" Ma yelled. She was trying to stop Papa from hurting Real Kill some more. Mr. Jabo lit his pipe. He seemed to be enjoying himself as much as Ralph was. I reckon he'd been wanting to give Real Kill a beating ever since Real Kill told Miss Lottie Pearl to shut up at Mr. King David's funeral.

Uncle Goat wasn't about to help his friend because he didn't want to mess up his clothes and horrible hairdo. He stood on the porch to make sure the slight rain that had started to fall didn't nappy his hair up.

"Jabo, make Stanbury stop before he kill that boy," Ma yelled, but Mr. Jabo ignored Ma and let Papa have his way with poor Real Kill. Papa rolled Real Kill over and picked him up by the seat of his britches and threw him a little farther in the grass.

"Stop it, Husband!" Ma screamed again, but Papa picked Real Kill up again and threw him some more.

Deacon Ward finally pulled Ralph away because he was on the ground like a referee, getting ready to count Real Kill out.

"Stop, stop, stop, ole man!" Real Kill hollered.

"N'all, boy. You need-need-need to be taught some manners."

"Somebody get this fool," Real Kill pleaded.

"Get-get off my land, boy," Papa shouted, "and don't you come back till you learn some manners." Papa knew good and well that we lived on the Wileys' land, not our own. He gave Real Kill one last lick for the road. Real Kill was too drunk and too beat-up to do anything except run down Low Meadows Lane. After he dashed off, everybody went inside as if nothing happened. Me, Ralph, and Pole stood there to see what the dignified folk would do next, but they were already saying good-bye.

Ma hung her head in shame at the way Papa had carried on. "Mr. Creecy, you and Mrs. Creecy come on in and see Mr. Bro. Wiley." Mrs. Creecy looked horrified. Mr. Creecy was trying his best not to laugh.

"We best get back to town before the storm comes," Mrs. Creecy told Ma.

"Don't you want a piece of apple pie?" Ma asked.

"Thank you, but we best be moving on. Besides, the wind seems to be picking up," Mr. Creecy said. The dignified folks went on about their business.

Nineteen

B ack in the house, Reverend Hornbuckle and
Miss Florenza were sitting with Mr. Bro.
Wiley's body like they were the National Guard. The
reverend never stopped chewing what had to be his fifth
piece of chicken. Wait till Ma see him eating in her living room.

"Folks, it's time for us to pay our last respects to Mr.
Bro. Wiley before the storm comes," Reverend Horn-
buckle said, standing up. We all gathered around Mr.
Bro. Wiley's casket and held hands. Ma rolled her eyes
at the reverend when he put his plate in the chair Mr.
Gordon brought over.

"Let us pray," the reverend said. We lowered our heads.

"Dear Lord, we need you every hour," Reverend

Hornbuckle prayed. Suddenly, a clap of thunder struck with a loud boom. So loud that it hurt my ears. The womenfolk jumped with fear. "Lord, we need you to come by here and bless this sittin' up. Bless the people who have gathered here to honor and praise Mr. Bro. Wiley."

Pole held my hand tight as the rain began to fall hard and the preacher prayed on.

"Pole, you cutting my blood off. Don't hold so tight."

"Shh," Ma said.

'Fore I could breathe another breath, Miss Lottie Pearl, who can't sing a lick, belted out a song.

"May the work I've done, speak for me. May the work I've done, speak for me."

I wondered why folk who can't sing don't know it.

"When I've done the best I can and my friends don't understand, may the work that I've done, speak for me," Ma joined in.

When they finished singing, Reverend Hornbuckle reached in his suit pocket, but came up empty.

"Anybody got a Bible?" he asked.

"Who ever saw a preacher man with no Bible," Ralph whispered to me. I looked at all the grown folk looking at Reverend Hornbuckle in disbelief.

"Why he don't have a Bible, Papa?" I asked.

"Bean, get-get the Bible," Papa said like he was mad

163

at me for asking a good question. I knew he couldn't be ashamed of me after the way he had just embarrassed Ma in front of company twenty minutes earlier. Surely not.

I reached in the dresser drawer behind me and gave him Mr. Bro. Wiley's Bible.

Ma had it wrapped in dead folk fabric just like everything that she thought was important.

"'Yea, though I walk through the valley of the shadow of death,'" Rev. Hornbuckle read.

Before he could even finish reading the Twenty-Third Psalm, Miss Lottie Pearl started singing again.

"Oh, Lottie Pearl, we didn't need another song," Miss Florenza said with a big laugh. Miss Florenza must have lost her mind telling Ma's best friend what to do in our house.

Pole's eyes got big 'cause she knew her mama was about to raise pure cane. Ralph's ears went up like a rabbit's. He was ready for another fight.

"Florenza, you got one more thing to say to me before you in that casket with Mr. Bro. Wiley," Miss Lottie Pearl told the sinner.

"Ain't nobody scared of you, woman."

"All right, ladies," Reverend Hornbuckle finally said. Before the womenfolk could fuss some more, the door flew wide-open and Real Kill came running back inside. He was wet as a duck and out of breath.

"Didn't I tell-tell you to stay out of my house?" Papa yelled.

Real Kill tried to stand up straight, but the liquor was still in him, so he held on to Ralph's shoulder.

"Man, listen to me. You got to listen," Real Kill pleaded.

"Let him talk, Husband," Ma said. "Something's got to be wrong."

"Speak fast, Real Kill. You best-best speak fast," Papa told him.

"The flood is coming. I just ran into Christian talking to Mr. Creecy. He was headed to his house to get his belongings. Folks in town told him the dam broke in Occoneechee Neck. Them folks headed into town where the land is high. He said that white folk told him the Low Meadows is gonna be underwater 'fore noon tomorrow. Said our dam might break! Mr. Creecy asked Mr. Christian to come and warn y'all 'cause he said I was too drunk. When Mr. Creecy left I promised Christian I would take care of this, so here I am. Here I am, Florenza."

We were so busy with the sittin' up nobody checked the river to see how high it was. But we knew if Mr. Creecy had sent word for us to get out of the Low Meadows it was time to go. Mr. Christian didn't care much for the colored folk, so I wondered if he would have told Real Kill to warn us if it were not for Mr. Creecy.

"Y'all know that river gets mad when it rains. It might run us out of here this time," Real Kill said.

"Shut up, Real Kill. You know good and well Christian don't talk to no colored folk," Miss Florenza said, laughing.

"Oh, sugar. I came back for you and you talking ugly to me. Why, baby? Why? Why you so mean to Real Kill?" he said as he tried to stand his tall lean body up straight. He tipped his hat on his narrow head, which was shaped just like Big Shot Bob's pea head.

Papa moved in between Real Kill and Miss Florenza. He put his hand on Real Kill's chest. Some of that liquor must have worn off because he looked down at Papa's hand and said, "Get your hands off me, Stanbury."

Ma gave Papa the Evil Eye that said don't beat on Real Kill no more. "Both of you, stop it. Children, get some ice for Real Kill's eye. Pole, fix him a plate. We need to finish the sittin' up and get out of these Low Meadows," Ma said. Real Kill's eye had grown twice the size it was before Papa punched him in it.

Ralph was following us and jabbing his fists in the air like he was ready for another fight. Pole wrapped the ice in the dead folk fabric that Ma had cut for a dish cloth and held it to Real Kill's head.

"I'll hold it. You fix Real Kill a plate," Ralph said. He would do anything to be near the action.

"Boy, I'm going to be a doctor. Why do I have to fix his plate?" Pole fussed.

I peeked out the window while Real Kill got his nursing and ate. I had never seen so much rain in my whole life. I believed that Ole River was sad that Mr. Bro. Wiley was dead and gone. It was time to get out of the Low Meadows for sure. The chickens had started to run about and the cows were trying to break the fence. Mule Bennett was banging on the barn door.

"Look at all that water. We need to get out of here," I said.

"I told you that ten minutes ago," Real Kill said. Ralph dropped the ice as he and Pole joined me at the window.

"Get your folks," Ralph told me, but he didn't have to say a word. I was already halfway to the sittin' up room.

Papa stood in the doorway.

"Come quick. The water rising," I whispered to him. Some of the menfolk saw Papa and Mr. Jabo leave the room. They followed, joining us in the kitchen. The womenfolk kept on praising the Lord along with Reverend Hornbuckle and a few men that stayed behind.

"Look, Papa. Look at the chickens and the cows. They moving up to high places 'cause they scared of the water. What we gonna do? What in the world we gonna do?" Pole cried.

"It's gonna be all right, baby, don't you worry," Mr. Jabo assured Pole.

"See, I told you it was time to go," Real Kill said, biting into another chicken leg.

"Stop eating my food, man. Y'all come with-with me," Papa said. "We got to save them animals and get these folk out of here."

Soon as Papa and the other menfolk went outside, me, Pole, and Ralph went right back to the window. Mr. Jabo and Uncle Goat measured the water with a stick.

"Come on, Jabo, we-we got to get them cows and Mule Bennett up to Stony Hill before they all drown," Papa said.

"I'm going with you," Uncle Goat told my papa.

Mr. Jabo and the men didn't say another word. They listened to my papa like folk in the Low Meadows always do. They knew my papa was a good man and smart too, even if he only had a second-grade education. They trusted him.

"I'll go to my store. We might need extra food," said Mr. Luther. He owned the only store in the Low Meadows. After the white man Mr. Coley closed his store we didn't have a place to shop for a whole year. Mr. Coley got tired fooling with us colored folk and left without saying a word. He was always mad with Ma and Miss Lottie Pearl because he didn't want coloreds touching stuff in the store unless they were gonna buy it. Ma was a peaceful woman but she would go in that store and try on hats just to let Mr. Coley know that what he was doing was wrong.

"Why is he back here in the Low Meadows with us colored folk if the store ain't for us?" Ma had told Papa.

"Gal, I'm gonna put the law on you if you put on one more hat," Mr. Coley once told Ma.

"Go ahead. And when you do, we gonna stop buying in your store and walk to Rich Square to get what we need from Mr. Taylor." After Ma said that, Miss Lottie Pearl grabbed an orange out the basket on the counter. She mashed that orange so hard that the juice squirted out. A little bit hit Mr. Coley right in the eye. That was the last straw for Mr. Coley. On Saturday, Miss Lottie Pearl was mashing oranges; come Monday morning, folk were walking six miles for a jug of milk. That's right. Mr. Coley closed his store while we were at church without saying one word. He did leave a note nailed on the front door.

CLOSED TO NIGGERS!
CLOSED PERIOD!
NOW MASH THAT ORANGE!

Mama and Miss Lottie Pearl was so happy they had told Mr. Coley off that they bragged for weeks. Papa and Mr. Jabo were not amused.

"You-you both could have been shot for trespassing!" Papa shouted.

"And we couldn't have done nothing about it!" Mr. Jabo added. I don't believe Mr. Coley had one intention of calling the law or shooting the womenfolk. He was sick of us and we were sick of him.

Sometimes colored folks just get tired, I reckon. Too tired to be scared.

It took a year, but Mr. Luther went around to all the colored in the Low Meadows each month until he had gathered enough money to buy the store. Folk gave him money they had been saving all their lives. Mr. Luther and Papa paid Mr. Coley a visit to discuss buying the store. Mr. Coley must have thought about that orange juice in his eye because he asked for Mr. Luther's mule too. Poor Papa and Mr. Luther had to walk all the way home. Papa's leg was swollen and hurting. Mr. Luther was sad that his mule was gone, but we were happy to have a store in the Low Meadows again.

Papa and the Low Meadows men would do anything for us. Saving our lives from the storm was no different.

"Come on with me, Real Kill. You can help me gather the food," Mr. Luther said.

I didn't want to think hard of Real Kill but I bet he

was hoping to get a little drink of liquor while he was at the store.

"Y'all be careful," Papa warned.

I guess he had forgiven Real Kill for talking bad to him. I reckon Real Kill had also forgiven Papa for beating the stuffing out of him.

Mr. Bro. Wiley used to tell us that hating and not forgiving folk will get you to hell quicker than any sickness. "Forgive those who treat you wrong. Your load in life will be lighter," the old slave told me.

"Deacon Ward, don't get too close, but you need to check the river. See how high it is. We gonna have to finish the sittin' up and leave here soon," Papa said.

"I'm going with my daddy," Ralph said and ran outside. Deacon Ward didn't send him back. My papa was right when he said Ralph became a man the day Deacon Ward let him stop going to school.

Then Papa came over to the window.

"Bean, I want you to go in the sittin' up room and tell your ma what's going on out here. Don't scare her. Tell her that the water is getting high and we can't wait till morning to leave. Tell Wife and Lottie Pearl to gather all the food they can. Tell the rest of the men-folk they need to get their boats ready." Then they all walked away.

Me and Pole went back to the sittin' up to tell the womenfolk that the flood was almost in the Low Meadows.

Mama looked in my eyes the way she did the night Mr. Bro. Wiley went to heaven.

"Where is Husband?" she asked.

I took Ma by her soft, fat hand and led her to the kitchen. Darkness had started to fall, so I pulled the curtain back and held the lantern to the window. Ma's face changed when she saw how high the water had risen.

"Lord, have mercy, Jesus. Help me if you please! Look at all that water." She turned to me. "Where did you say Husband went?"

"Papa, Mr. Stanbury, and Goat gone to get the cows moved up to Stony Hill," Pole answered.

"Real Kill and Mr. Luther gone to save the food in the store, while Deacon Ward and Ralph went to see how high the river is. Papa left me in charge," I said, 'cause that's how I felt at that very minute.

"You doing good, Bean. You doing real good," Ma said.

"Mr. Stanbury said for us to tell you and the other grown folk to get ready to leave here," Pole said. "He said to tell the menfolk to get their boats ready and for you and my ma to gather up food."

Ma left the room while Pole was still talking. We followed her to warn the Low Meadows folks that trouble had come to us.

TWENTY

Reverend Hornbuckle, I don't mean to take over the sittin' up 'cause I know you in charge, but I'm afraid the water is coming faster than we can finish praising Mr. Bro. Wiley," Ma said.

"Have mercy on us," Reverend Hornbuckle said.

Ma's eyes went all the way around the room.

"Ole River madder than it has ever been and it's about to swallow the Low Meadows just like Real Kill told us."

"Lord, Lord," Miss Lottie Pearl said.

"Husband said we best send the rest the men to get their boats. We gonna have to leave here long before morning."

Miss Florenza started crying, and for the first time in two years I saw her pay Sara some attention.

"Come here, baby."

"Ain't no need to cry. The Lord will make a way," Reverend Hornbuckle said.

"Yes, the Lord will make a way out of no way, but right now y'all men need to go and get your boats and tie them as high as you can to the trees in the front yard. That way when the water starts to rise, the boats will float to the top," Ma told us.

It wasn't a man in the Meadows that didn't have a homemade boat. Not one. Even though Ole River stole our ancestors, the men were drawn to the water to fish.

"Let's all say a few words for our beloved Mr. Bro. Wiley 'fore we leave this room," Reverend Hornbuckle said, turning to us. The other menfolk began to leave.

One by one the folk from the Low Meadows said something nice about Mr. Bro. Wiley.

"I'm sho' gonna miss our long talks," Miss Lottie Pearl said.

"I will miss you too," Miss Katie Mae added and cried with the womenfolk.

After most folk were done talking, Miss Florenza said her peace.

"Mr. Bro. Wiley, you been mighty good to us. You loved me more than anybody back here in the Low Meadows."

Miss Lottie Pearl just could not take it another minute.

"Hush up, Florenza. You think every man in the world in love with you. Even the dead! Now hush your fuss."

Miss Lottie Pearl might not have liked what Miss Florenza said but it was the truth. Mr. Bro. Wiley did love Miss Florenza. He loved everybody. We were down at the river one day when we saw the sinner going in her house.

"You know, Bean, for a woman to wear red every day that God sends, she crying for attention. We got to love and pray for Miss Florenza no matter what folk say. She just looking for love." Mr. Bro. Wiley was always a man whose words made sense. Even what he said about Miss Florenza sounded right to me.

"Ladies, ladies, let us have order. Mrs. Jones, would you please say the final words over Mr. Bro. Wiley?" Reverend Hornbuckle asked.

"Yes, Reverend, I believe I will."

Ma looked at Mr. Bro. Wiley like she ain't never been so hurt in her life. With her head down and arms crossed in front of her, Ma took a deep breath.

"Take your time, Sister, take your time," Miss Lottie Pearl said. Then she moved closer to Ma with the smelling salts. The other women stood around Ma to make sure she didn't fall out.

"Well, Mr. Bro. Wiley, this is the end of the road for us. I've known you all of my life and you was a good man. You helped those who needed help no matter the cost. I remember the time Miss Ida Bea's boy Frog got sick and nobody knew what to do for him. Nobody but you, Mr. Bro. Wiley. Nobody but you. You told Husband to go out to town and get that boy. 'Bring him here to me. Bring him to the Low Meadows,' you said.

"You sat up with Frog all night long, singing them old slave songs and praying for that child. I watched you rub him down in 'bacco leaves all night. Folk back here in the Low Meadows thought you were crazy, but not me, Mr. Bro. Wiley. Not me. You had special gifts from God. Your eyes saw what we couldn't see. I hope you went to heaven knowing that you been like a papa to me. I'm gonna miss you. Husband will miss you. Bean gonna miss you too. You been on this earth one hundred years and I know you tired. You being tired don't stop us from missing you though. You rest now. Rest all you want to, Mr. Bro. Wiley. Rest on."

Ma put her hands out like she was getting ready to play patty-cakes. She jumped up and down. She went around in circles. Ma stomped her feet. She went around in circles some more and spoke in tongues. Not to be outdone, Miss Lottie Pearl got to shouting too. The other women all joined in. Miss Katie Mae did everything except a cartwheel, while Miss Moszella screamed, "Hallelujah!" Reverend Hornbuckle prayed again while the women calmed down and started humming "Precious Lord."

"Lord, in this final hour we have come to say goodbye to Mr. Bro. Wiley. Let his soul rest in peace."

"That was one fast prayer," Pole whispered to me.

"It sho' was. I'm kinda glad though. We got to get out of here before Ole River get sick of the womenfolk shouting and come on in the house."

When they were done, the women went in the kitchen and started putting the food into wood crates. Pole helped wrap the biscuits in wax paper. The womenfolk gathered some dead folk fabric and stuffed the corners of the house to slow the water down, while I watched for Papa and the other menfolk.

Soon they came back in the house as wet as the chickens outside. Ma gave the men some dead folk fabric out of the trunk to dry themselves off.

"Husband, did you save the animals? Did you get Mule Bennett moved to Stony Hill?"

"Yes, we did," Papa said as Deacon Ward and Ralph came inside.

"The water is getting higher by the minute. We will never make it out of here with the women and children. I don't know how long we gonna be safe in this house," Deacon Ward said.

Papa looked at the ceiling.

"We gonna have to cut a hole in the roof. We might have to climb on top of the house before morning," he said.

"That roof ain't nothing but two layers of tin. Can't hold everybody. We can make it, Husband," Ma said.

"Let's try to get out now."

"It's too-too late, Wife. The water is too strong for the boats. We can't see no further than our hands. We got to-to stay here till morning," Papa said.

"Can we make it to Stony Hill?" Miss Lottie Pearl asked Mr. Jabo.

"Afraid not, Lottie Pearl. The wind too high. It might blow all the windows out of the house 'cause it's sitting so high off the ground."

"Lord, help us," Miss Lottie Pearl said. I tried to keep it together and trust Papa. Mr. Bro. Wiley said fear and God can't live under the same roof, so I kept trying not to be scared.

"All right, folks," Papa said, "the water done rose all the way to the steps. We know what we got to do. We can't leave Mr. Bro. Wiley's body back here to float away. Besides, Magnolia with-with child and she can't get all-all worked up."

"Well, amen," I whispered to Pole. "Somebody finally admitted that Ma gonna have a baby that I didn't ask for."

That tickled Pole for just a minute, but then she went back to worrying about the storm. I was some kind of worried too, but I kept thinking about how Ma said it was time for me to be a man. Besides, if Papa was in charge I felt everything would be all right.

"What we gonna do till morning?" Miss Florenza asked.

"Pray," Reverend Hornbuckle said. "We gonna pray."

"Help us, Lord," Miss Katie Mae cried out.

"Yes, Lord. Please help us," Miss Florenza said. Miss Lottie Pearl rolled her eyes at Miss Florenza. Poor Miss Florenza can't even talk to Jesus without Miss Lottie Pearl putting her two cents in.

Papa grabbed Ma's hand.

"Finish gathering the-the food, Wife, and get the children ready." Papa hugged her tight.

"Reckon Luther and Real Kill all right?" Ma asked Papa.

"Luther know-knows these roads like the back of his hand," Papa said.

I listened to the grown folk and I thought about Mr. Bro. Wiley.

"Bean?" Pole said.

"Yes."

"Do you remember what Mr. Bro. Wiley told us about the river getting mad one day and rising up?" It was just like Pole to be thinking my very thoughts.

"I remember. I think Mr. Bro. Wiley was right. If we don't make it out of these Low Meadows, I want you to know that you my best friend in the world."

"You my best friend too," Pole said.

We held hands. "But you know what I really think?" I

said. "I think Ole River and Mr. Bro. Wiley were friends like me and you. He said he and the river knew things that nobody but God knew. They had secrets like we got secrets. Ole River mad that his friend is gone."

"I hope Ole River ain't too mad, Bean, 'cause we too young to die."

I didn't say a word 'cause Ma told me that death don't have a number. She said death comes when it wants and for who it wants. I stopped listening to Pole so that I could hear what Papa was saying.

I tried to listen, but my heart was some kind of heavy with the thought of death. I wanted to see Mr. Bro. Wiley again someday in heaven, but not at twelve years old. I just kept my eyes on Papa to run the fear away from my heart.

"We gonna cut a hole in the ceiling so we can put the women and children on the roof," Papa said to Mr. Jabo. "Goat, see if you can knock a hole in the ceiling with the hammer while I swim to the barn to get the ladder."

"You can't go out there, Husband," Ma said.

"I got to go. I got to go, Wife." When he opened the door, water came rushing in the house. Papa stepped out with no hesitation and disappeared into the darkness while Uncle Goat tried to knock a hole in the ceiling, but it was just too high to reach without the ladder.

Papa swam all the way to the barn as everybody

watched. Ralph looked on with excitement. That boy had something crazy inside of him that made him crave the dangerous side of life. What most folk feared made him smile.

While Papa was gone, I ran to my room and looked around just in case Ole River took my home away from me. I wanted to see it one last time. I opened the drawer and grabbed the picture of Mr. Bro. Wiley's mama and the slave papers. I put his pocket watch in a old candy bag to make sure it did not get wet. When I got back to the kitchen, Papa had the ladder and saw under his arm. He was some kind of wet and tired. I was proud of my papa. I only wished I could help more.

"Don't fall, Papa," I said as he climbed the ladder.

"Son, hand me a piece of stove wood." I reached in the wood crate beside the potbelly stove and got Papa the biggest piece of wood I could find. Papa used the wood to finish knocking a hole in the ceiling. Then he used the saw to make it even bigger.

"The-the Lord gonna let up-up on the rain sooner or-or later. When he do, we-we got to get the womenfolk up on the roof with the children," Papa told Mr. Jabo.

"What about you and the other men?" Pole asked Mr. Jabo.

"We gonna be fine. We can stand on the high furniture. Goat, get the table and pull it close," Mr. Jabo told my uncle. Mr. Jabo was trying to be the boss like Papa.

"Well, what about Mr. Bro. Wiley?" Pole asked. All the grown folk looked at her as if she had cursed. I didn't know why. It sounded like a good question to me. Grown folk think they so smart. I wanted to see them figure that one out. Papa finally spoke up.

"Jabo, we-we don't have no-no choice. We got to make-make this hole bigger and-and put Mr. Bro. Wiley on the roof with the women and children. Then we-we need to lay some boards across the beams to make sure the roof don't fall-fall in."

This time Mr. Jabo climbed up on the ladder. I was getting ready to give him a piece of wood to make the hole bigger, but Pole beat me to the wood box. She wanted to help her daddy the way I wanted to help mine. The wood was heavy, but Pole picked it up like she was a grown man. Without gloves! Mr. Jabo smiled at her.

"Thank you, baby girl."

Mr. Jabo had a strange look on his face when he climbed down from the ladder.

"The rain letting up, Stanbury, but Ole River getting higher. I need a lantern to see better, but I believe the other dam just broke. We best get folk on top of the house right now."

Ma started giving everybody a piece of dead folk fabric to cover their heads. I didn't want that mess. The only time I wanted to be near that cloth was when I was lying on a piece, dead and gone, and I had no plans of dying that night.

"I-I need one man to go up on the roof with the women to make sure they all right," Papa said.

Before anybody else could volunteer, the preacher man stepped up. "I'll go."

"He going where the food going," Pole whispered to me.

"All right, Reverend-Reverend Hornbuckle, you go-go first. When you get-get up there, I'm gonna-gonna start helping the children up the ladder. You got-got to pull them up with care now."

"Papa. Let me go on up with Reverend Hornbuckle. I can help him with the women and children," I said.

"All right, Bean," Papa said as Deacon Ward turned to Ralph.

"Come on, son, we need to close Mr. Bro. Wiley's casket and get him ready to go on the roof."

Ralph walked ahead of his father without even asking for the lantern.

There was something about Ralph that made me respect him even more that night. Some of the kids at school used to call him slow, but the truth was he had heart! In that heart, there was no fear. He had learned what it meant to be a man long before his time.

Reverend Hornbuckle stood on the table as the men started to push him up the ladder. He had almost made it when I heard a sound like a piece of paper tearing. Poor fellow. The reverend almost fell off the ladder grabbing his pants as they split right down the middle. Lord knows I tried not to laugh, but no one could hold it in. Even Ma lost her kind spirit for a minute and laughed too. Reverend Hornbuckle kept on going as his white drawers peeped down at us. When they finally got the big preacher man on the roof, Papa helped me through the hole.

"You all right, Reverend Hornbuckle?" I asked.

"Just praying, son!" I looked towards the barn. The chickens were all the way on the top of the hen house. Not one was trying to fly away. Reckon even a chicken got enough sense to be scared.

TWENTY-ONE

Papa, hand me a lantern," I said as I reached down into the kitchen.

"Here, put this saucer over the lantern so the fire will not go out," Ma said as she passed a piece of Depression glass to me.

The light shined on Mama's face. She looked proud of me. Right then I knew what it was to be a Low Meadows man. I was helping take care of my people.

With the lantern in hand, I could see Reverend Hornbuckle's face. I saw fear in his eyes that I ain't never seen in no man. The sounds we could hear from up on the roof scared us all. We could hear the small waves of water coming for us both. The tree branches were snapping and the cows got louder. I listened for Mule

Bennett, but he never made a sound. I feared he had gone on to hev'n with Mr. Bro. Wiley.

"Great God Almighty! The water coming! Save us, Lord," Reverend Hornbuckle shouted.

"Papa, Papa, we got to hurry. Ole River mad as hell. We got to get the womenfolk up here right now."

"Bean, is you cursing?" Ma yelled through the hole.

"Sorry, Ma." I reached down for Pole as she climbed up the ladder. Sara was right behind her, crying to beat the band. Since Ma was carrying the next Low Meadows baby, she came up after the children. Miss Lottie Pearl came on the roof next. Then poor Miss Moszella, who was out of breath, climbed up. I kept praying the roof wouldn't fall in.

"What you see now, Bean?" Papa asked. I stuck my head down in the kitchen. Papa was standing on a chair with water around his ankles. The menfolk had moved Mr. Bro. Wiley's casket to the kitchen table. Ralph never left his papa's side.

"Water, Papa, water. I see water everywhere. The Ole River getting higher." I looked out into the Low Meadows and the water was touching the bottom leaves on the willow trees. That's when I heard a loud bang near the barn.

"What was that, Bean?" Mr. Jabo asked.

"Reverend Hornbuckle's car slamming against the barn." I held the lantern up high. I could see the coupe much better. Mr. Taylor's truck was floating towards the barn too.

"Bean, move everybody back. We got to make room for Mr. Bro. Wiley just in case the men have to swim up to Stony Hill. The roof can't hold us all. If we have to go to Stony Hill, you in charge. You hear me, Son?"

"Yes, Papa, I hear you." Seem like all my fear went away when Papa said I was in charge.

"Fear and God can't stay in the same house," Mr. Bro. Wiley said to me time and time again.

"Okay, I'm gonna count to three and I need everybody to push," Papa said.

"Move back," Mr. Jabo yelled.

Me and Reverend Hornbuckle pulled the casket as hard as we could while the menfolk pushed it from the other side. Ain't no "*man*" in Reverend Hornbuckle. He was breathing like it was the end of his life.

"Easy now, easy," Papa said.

"Come on, Mr. Bro. Wiley. Come on," I said as I pulled the casket up on the rooftop.

It seemed as if Mr. Bro. Wiley wasn't even inside anymore. Like he'd already floated to heaven. Light and free!

When we got the casket on the roof, we pushed him near the womenfolk. Ma laid her head on the casket like it was a pillow while the rain came down on her face. Miss Lottie Pearl laid her head on the other side.

It wasn't long before the Lord sent a blessing and the rain stopped. Other than the lanterns, which I covered with dead folk fabric, the Low Meadows was dark and you could hear a pin drop. We just sat there with Mr. Bro. Wiley's casket. We prayed. Every now and then one of the womenfolk would start singing.

"*I want to be at the meeting. I want to be at the meeting,*" I heard coming from the back of the roof.

I turned around and couldn't believe my eyes.

"It's Miss Florenza," I told Pole.

"*I want to be at the meeting,*" she sang louder. Then I heard voices coming from the kitchen. I peeked in the big hole. I could barely see the menfolk standing on the table and in the chairs holding hands like little children at the schoolhouse. They were doing some singing too.

"*When I get to hev'n, I'll meet my mother there. Great God Almighty, here comes my child.*"

I soon fell asleep listening to their voices.

TWENTY-TWO

I woke up first. Then Pole.

"Mornin', Pole. We're still alive," I said as she rubbed her eyes. We looked out at the Low Meadows. The place Ma and Papa said would always be home was under muddy water. So high that you could hardly see the small barn in the backyard that Papa built with his own hands.

"I can't see no land," Pole said.

"It ain't gone, Pole. Everything just covered up. Ole River can't stay mad forever. It'll go back down and we will live here again."

"The hen house! The chickens! The chickens," Pole screamed. I stood up and looked out at the Low Meadows.

"They dead," I whispered as Ma woke up and Sara screamed real loud.

"Don't look, child," Miss Florenza told her. She pulled Sara closer to her. Ma and Miss Lottie Pearl needed to leave Miss Florenza be. She loved her child same as they loved us.

Ma looked over at Stony Hill.

We could see Mule Bennett and four cows that survived. All of Mr. Thomas's cows but four had drowned.

"What's going on up there?" Papa said. I put my head down in the hole to give Papa a report. I thanked God that our house was on a small hill too because the trees outside were almost underwater, but the men were fine on the tables.

"Most of the animals are dead, Papa."

"Figured as-as much," he said as he looked up at me to assure me that everything would be all right. He and the other men were so wet and coughing from the chill the night before.

"Y'all get back. We can't open the door. We coming up on the roof to get to the boats," Papa said. He climbed on the roof, but never stopped. He jumped right in the water.

Papa and Mr. Jabo swam towards the boats.

"Hurry out of the water. Dead chickens in there and most of the cows dead. I reckon disease in that water by now," Ma shouted.

My uncle might be a liar, but he had good in him just like Mr. Bro. Wiley said every man had. He forgot all about his greasy head of hair and jumped in the water too. One by one the other menfolk jumped in and got their small boats. Next thing I knew Ralph was right beside Deacon Ward swimming like a fish. Ma looked away for one minute and it was my chance to join them.

I jumped in the water with my arms up high like the great sprinter Mr. Jesse Owens. Ralph pumped his fist up in the air when he saw me swimming towards him. We smiled at each other.

"Come back here, Bean," Ma yelled.

I had never disobeyed Ma in my whole life but I had to help. We gathered the boats and headed back to get everyone.

"Women and-and children first," Papa said as they got closer to the house with the boats.

"Jump, child. We got to hurry," Mr. Jabo said as he reached out for Pole.

"Close your eyes real tight, Pole. Don't look," I told her.

Pole did like I said and jumped into her papa's arms.

Ma forgot all about being mad at me and she smiled something big at me holding the boat steady while folk climbed in.

Mr. Jabo reached out for Sara. "Come on, child. Everything gonna be all right." Then she jumped in his arms.

"Sit down, Sara. Let the women get in now," Mr. Jabo said. One by one, the women got into the boats with help from the menfolk. Uncle Goat pulled his boat up last.

My uncle got a nice boat, and they were saving it for Mr. Bro. Wiley's casket.

"God knew what he was doing when he sent that rain early last night. If the weather was good we would have had a house full of folk," Reverend Hornbuckle said to us.

"Ain't-ain't that the truth," Papa said. "Now let's get Mr. Bro. Wiley on the boat and get out of these Meadows."

"Push one time. Push hard," Papa told Uncle Goat, who was back on the roof to get the casket.

Ma was crying harder than Pole when the casket hit the bottom of the boat.

"Oh, Wife, don't cry." Papa said.

"I know but I wanted Mr. Bro. Wiley's sittin' up to be nice. Look how things done turned out."

"Stop your crying now, and get in the boat with Mr. Bro. Wiley if you want to," Uncle Goat told his sister, motioning for her to get in the boat with him. Then he swapped places with Papa.

"Bean, you look out for the folks in our boat," Papa said.

Ma wrapped her funeral fabric around her shoulders

and stood up. When she got ready to get in the boat with Mr. Bro. Wiley, she held her belly and let out a scream.

"Husband, baby's coming!"

"Not now, Wife, not now!" Papa took Ma's hand and helped her get in the boat with him and Mr. Bro. Wiley.

What in the world was Papa talking about! He knew good and well he couldn't stop a baby from coming.

"Lord, Sister, you done got too excited. This baby ain't due for another three weeks. Slide that casket over and make room for me and Moszella," Miss Lottie Pearl told Papa.

"Ain't enough room in here for Moszella and the casket," Papa said.

Miss Moszella rolled her eyes at my papa.

"Ain't nobody studyin' you, Stanbury Jones."

"Get in this boat, Florenza. You don't weigh even one hundred pounds, so you got to help me bring this baby into the world," Miss Lottie Pearl said.

"Me? No way," she shouted. "I would rather die."

"Don't push your luck, gal. Now, get your hind parts in this boat," Miss Lottie Pearl ordered the sinner.

"Stanbury, you best move us behind the barn, out of the sight of the children and the menfolk, 'cause we ain't gonna make it to town. You remember how quick Bean came into the world," Ma said as she struggled for each breath, sweating like she was in the 'bacco field.

Miss Lottie Pearl was busy taking all our dead folk fabric from us like she was taking up collection in church. She stuffed the fabric around the boat so that Ma could lie down.

"Jabo, don't know how long we gonna be, you all best go on without us," Papa said.

"Stanbury Jones, we have seen the worst of times together. I ain't leaving you back here. We gonna stay right here till this child come in this world. Go on now."

Papa, Ma, Miss Lottie Pearl, and Mr. Bro. Wiley's casket disappeared behind the barn with Miss Florenza. We could hear Ma screaming. The sinner screamed every time Ma screamed.

I wondered what in the world was going on. Surely Ma was going to be all right. I was some kind of curious and worried about what was happening to her.

"I sure hope Miss Magnolia be all right," Pole said.

"Well, it hurts to bring a child into the world, just like it hurt when someone leave here, child," Reverend Hornbuckle said.

TWENTY-THREE

An hour passed. Though everyone tried to comfort me, I was still worried. I was mainly upset that Cousin Babe wasn't with us to bring the baby into the world. She had birthed every colored baby in this town. Folk said Cousin Babe had a special gift from God for delivering. I wondered if Miss Lottie Pearl knew enough to help my ma.

Pole touched my knee.

"Don't worry, Bean. Ma and Mr. Stanbury ain't gonna let nothing happen to Miss Magnolia."

"That's right, child, don't worry. Let's pray for the new baby and your mother," Reverend Hornbuckle said. He started praying real loud so that we would drown out Ma's screams.

We sang some more as the sun got hotter. The mosquitoes were trying to pick us up and carry us away, but we kept right on singing. A whole hour passed.

"Here they come, Bean. Here they come," Pole said, jumping for joy.

"'The Lord giveth and the Lord taketh away,'" Reverend Hornbuckle said.

Ma was barely sittin' up in the boat, but I was so glad to see her.

"It's a boy, Bean," she said in a weak voice as I climbed out of the boat into theirs to get a better peep at my new little brother. He was a fine-looking little fellow and he was yellow like Ma. His eyes were wide-open like he had been around a long time. Poor baby boy. Ma had him all wrapped in that pink dead folk fabric that she gave me last night. Papa had a big smile on his face. I wasn't jealous or nothing, I just wondered if he was smiling the same way when I was born twelve years ago. I bet he was.

"Let's get out of these Low Meadows 'fore Ole River decide to come after us again," Papa said. Reverend Hornbuckle gave Mr. Jabo his pocket knife so that he could cut the other boats from the trees. What the reverend doing with a knife was beyond me. Maybe he and Miss Florenza belonged together after all. She smoked and he carried a knife just like any other man.

"Miss Magnolia, what you gonna name the baby?" Pole asked.

"His name is Wiley. Wiley Stanbury Jones."

"That's real nice, Ma," I said, still trying to get a closer look at my new little brother. Holding Baby Wiley with one hand, Ma put her other hand on Mr. Bro. Wiley's casket. I wondered if Ma was planning to tell my little brother that he was born in a boat with a dead man.

"Hold the boats!" Papa said as he rowed in front of us to lead us down Low Meadows Lane.

My heart was hurting for the land and the animals that we left behind.

Twenty-Four

T hank you, God, for bringing us this far by faith," the reverend said as he watched his coupe float towards the river.

"Amen," Miss Moszella said, swatting the mosquito that had just bit her fat arm. Sara's laugh rang out like a little bird at the sight of Miss Moszella beating the poor insect to death. Her smile was pretty and her eyes twinkled.

"We safe, Ma," she said to Miss Florenza.

"Not yet, but we will be soon. We almost out of here, baby."

My eyes fell on the sad sight of the Low Meadows. The cows were floating like paper, and the chickens were so light they had washed down to Ole River. Most of the leaves had fallen from the oak trees. The willows appeared sadder looking with all the mud stuck to the leaves.

All was silent until we heard Mr. Christian yelling for help. I followed the sound until I saw him on top of his house.

"Don't leave me back here. Please don't leave me back here."

"We coming to get you," Mama said in a weak voice.

"Why we helping him, Ma? He don't care about us."

"Oh, Bean, that ain't the way to act. We all God's children," Miss Dora Mae said from the boat beside us.

Ma gave me that "I'm going to tear your tail up" look.

Mr. Jabo stopped paddling his boat so that he could pick up our neighbor. Mr. Christian's face was as white as a bed sheet and his eyes were filled with water.

"Get in-in," Papa said to Mr. Christian.

"Thank you," he said, holding on to a brown leather bag. His blond hair was stuck to his head and his expensive white-folk clothes were wet and dirty.

"What you doing still back here? Real Kill said you left last night," Miss Lottie Pearl blurted out.

"I came back to get a few more things, but the car engine flooded. I tried to make it to Stanbury's house, but it was too late."

"What's in the bag?" Miss Lottie Pearl asked.

"For God's sake, stay out that man's business," Mr. Jabo told his nosy wife.

I know it was killing Miss Lottie Pearl not to say anything else, but she shut up as we headed out of the Low Meadows. Her eyes were glued to the tree branches, plows, and animals all floating in the water. The menfolk had to row hard to keep the boats headed away from the river, where all the animals had floated.

"Look!" Pole screamed and pointed towards Mr. Luther's store. A body was floating towards us. Ole River done killed somebody.

"Jabo, stop for the body, but let the other boats keep going," Papa yelled. That suited me just fine. Don't reckon I wanted to see another dead person, but I peeped anyway.

"That's Real Kill," Ralph shouted.

He was right because I could see Real Kill's boots that Papa gave him last year when all the sharecroppers got a new pair. Mr. Thomas had fired Real Kill because he stayed drunk all the time, so Papa gave him his boots. Like most folks Mr. Thomas felt sorry for the town drunk, so he let him stay in the house but never let him work again.

"I wonder where in the world Luther is," Ma said to Papa as Mr. Jabo and Deacon Ward put poor Real Kill in the boat and covered him with the dead folk fabric.

"Wherever he-he is, he's alive. He know-know how to

survive. No, sir, Ole River didn't kill Luther," Papa said, looking around.

"Over there," Mr. Jabo said, pointing at the store. Mr. Luther was sitting on the roof, not even calling out for help. He was just crying like a baby. Mr. Jabo rowed his boat to the store and helped Mr. Luther get in. Mr. Luther wiped his tears with the end of Ma's dead folk fabric, then he started pulling food out of his bag.

"Here, Pole, pass out these crackers," Mr. Luther said as he reached over and gave her the bag. Pole gave us four crackers each. She was some kind of proud to be helping Mr. Luther.

"How did he die, Luther?" Miss Lottie Pearl finally asked.

"Died just like he lived. He kept that liquor bottle to his mouth all the way to the store. By the time we got here, he was drunk as a skunk. After I gathered the food and we were outside, Real Kill went back in the store for more liquor. I told him to stay with me but he went back anyway. When Real Kill came out, the water was really high. That boy ain't never known how to swim. Next thing I knew he was crying for help. I tried to save him. God knows I did. I told him to take my hand and hold on while I pull him on the roof. He was too drunk. He wasn't listening."

Mr. Luther put his white-haired head down and cried

like I ain't never seen a grown man cry before. I knew it hurt him not to be able to save a man's life. That sho' would have hurt me.

We kept on going down Low Meadows Lane in the water that Ole River left behind. It wasn't long before I heard a noise that sounded like a car, but it was too loud to be a car. There was no way anybody could drive in all that water. The noise got louder and louder. That's when we saw it! The biggest boat I had ever seen in my life.

COAST GUARD was written on the front and along the side.

"A boat! They coming to help us!" Pole yelled out. All the men were white except one.

"A colored man! Mr. Creecy! Our hope!"

"Hey, Mr. Creecy," we all shouted, his tall frame towering over the other men.

"Good morning!" he said as the boat slowed down, splashing water all over us.

"Stanbury, anyone else back there?" Mr. Creecy asked.

"I think we got everybody, but it wouldn't hurt to double check," Papa told him.

"What about the animals? Where is Mule Bennett?" he asked my papa. Mr. Creecy knew how much we thought of our mule.

"He on Stony Hill with the four cows that survived."

"Go on into town. They got water and food for

everyone. I can't bring Mule Bennett out on this boat, but we'll leave some food for him and the cows."

"I sho' thank you-you," Papa told him.

"Bye, Mr. Creecy!" we all shouted.

"You was right, Papa."

"Right about what, child?"

"Mr. Creecy is our hope," I said.

"God is our-our real hope, child. He will always send his angels. Always."

We were on our way again when I saw some folk in a tiny fishing boat.

"I believe that's Sue and her boy," Ma said as she tried her best to sit up in the boat. They were alone like always in a little old fishing boat. Miss Sue's two-timing husband, Michael, ran off with Miss Lottie Pearl's sister, Lita, two springs earlier. To make matters worse, Miss Lottie Pearl and Miss Lita were Miss Sue's first cousins on their ma's side. Miss Lottie Pearl did some talking about other folk, but she didn't ever mention her sister taking her own cousin's husband. No one said so, but I knew because Miss Lita had come home from Philadelphia that spring. When she left, Michael Flowers left too. Grown folk acted like he was dead and ain't mentioned him since then. He ain't dead because there was no sittin' up.

After Mr. Flowers left, Miss Sue kept on doing what

she had to do for herself and Grady. I believe she was sick of that man anyhow. He was courting every woman that he could find. I heard Miss Lottie Pearl say he wouldn't hit a lick at a black snake. That's just how lazy he was.

I looked at Grady and his mama out there in the water with nobody to help them. Mr. Flowers should be ashamed of himself. Uncle Goat took a rope from his boat and tied Miss Sue's little fishing boat to ours and we continued on to town.

"Thank you for helping us, Stanbury. We could hear that coast guard boat, but when we got round front of my house they were gone. We slept in this boat all night," Miss Sue said.

"You-you safe now," Papa told her.

Grady smiled at Pole.

Wasn't no need for him to even look at Pole. If she ever went to the dance with anybody from the Low Meadows, it would surely be me.

Everyone headed towards town where the white folk were. The farther we got, the lower the water got. Some folk were wading in the waist-deep water. Some folk were riding in their boats.

"Papa, there go Cousin Braxton and Cousin Babe. And he got Cousin Mer and Pattie Mae," I said, glad that they'd made it safely to us.

"Barb Jean and Coy with them too," Ralph said. He

was glad to see Coy because he was a good boxer. Ralph liked him a lot.

"Hey, y'all," I said.

"Hey, Pattie Mae," Pole said. Pole looked like she was some kind of glad to see Pattie Mae. She was older than Pattie Mae, but they loved to play together when she came to the Low Meadows.

"Hey, everybody," Pattie Mae said.

Cousin Braxton pulled his boat up beside Papa's.

"Y'all all right?"

"We fine. You folks all right?" Papa asked.

"We're fine, Stanbury. I'm sorry we didn't make it to the sittin' up last night. Babe made some coconut pies, but the clouds looked so bad I thought we best stay on Rehoboth Road."

"You-you did the right thing," Papa told Cousin Braxton. "We would have been-been in trouble sho' 'nuf if more than-than Low Meadows folk had been at the sittin' up. We wouldn't have had-had enough boats." Papa was quiet for a minute before saying, "We lost Real Kill."

"Lord, have mercy," Cousin Mer said.

Baby Wiley let out a cry. He sounded like a little cat. I don't believe Cousin Mer or Cousin Babe had noticed the new baby before he cried.

"Gal, you done had that baby?" Cousin Babe said as her face lit up.

"Yes, ma'am. I had him this morning. Lottie Pearl remembered everything you showed her from when Bessie's girl was born last fall."

"I helped," Miss Florenza said with a big grin on her face. Miss Babe didn't even look at Miss Florenza. I heard her tell Ma last year that she was gonna tell Miss Florenza a piece of her mind if she ever came on Rehoboth Road carrying on with the menfolk the way she do down in the Low Meadows.

"Hand him to me," Cousin Babe said, still ignoring poor Miss Florenza. Cousin Braxton struggled to get his boat close to us so his wife could get Baby Wiley.

"He is one fine baby," she said. Then she sang "Jesus Loves Me" to my new little brother.

TWENTY-FIVE

A whole hour passed before we made it to the town square. The water was so low that the men got out and started pulling the boats the rest of the way. Ralph and Coy helped. I wanted to join them but I needed to be near Ma since Papa was helping pull the boats in. I wanted to comfort her. Take care of her like a man.

"Ma, Ole River seemed madder at us colored folk than the white folk."

"Why in the world would you think such a thing?" Ma asked as she tried to nurse Baby Wiley without showing her breast. She pulled the dead folk fabric tight as I looked the other way.

"They don't have much water out here and ain't nobody dead."

"Son, I believe Ole River is like God. Color don't matter at all."

Ma stopped talking to me 'cause she was looking at Miss Remie's big house, which sat right on the edge of town.

"Lord, Husband, stop the boat. That's Miss Remie."

There she was. One of the richest white women in town, sitting all alone with water all the way to the tip of her porch.

"Why you sitting here, Miss Remie? Where is Mr. Faison?" Ma asked.

"I sent Jack into town with the car so he could put it on high land. I didn't think the water would get this close to my house. When it started to rise I came out here to wait for you. I knew you would come. I knew you would come."

"Waiting for me? Lord, have mercy, Miss Remie, you could have been killed."

Ma thought for a minute.

"Now, Miss Remie, you can always buy another car. You had no business staying here."

That white woman looked at all of us, one by one, then back at Ma.

"You are my only friend, Magnolia. You are my only friend."

Ma turned to me and put Baby Wiley in my arms. I held my little brother for the first time.

"He looks like us, Ma," I said as Wiley's eyes were opening and closing like he was sleepy.

They helped Miss Remie in the boat, and Ma held her tight.

Miss Lottie Pearl reached in her Sunday-go-to-meeting bag and gave Miss Remie a piece of dead folk fabric to wipe the sweat off her forehead. That touched my heart even if Miss Remie didn't show Mr. Faison the respect he deserved.

Pole smiled at her mama.

"Thank you, Lottie Pearl," Miss Remie said.

When we got to Main Street, we could see everyone making their way to Taylor's Grocery Store. Mr. Taylor was giving folk orange juice, sardines, and crackers.

White folk and the coloreds were all together that morning. The color of our skin didn't mean nothing. It didn't mean nothing at all. Everybody was just glad to be alive. The white women were crying just like our colored women.

When everyone saw the Low Meadows men pulling boats and wading in the water, they all noticed Mr. Bro. Wiley's casket and lowered their heads to show respect. The men removed their hats and the womenfolk cried some more. I hoped they wouldn't see Real Kill's body. That would have upset them for sure.

Sheriff Franklin was standing in the middle of the road telling folk where to tie their boats.

"Over there, Stanbury. Take your boats and tie them to the trees at the sawmill. Leave one man at each boat until we can get some order around here."

"What about Mr. Bro. Wiley's casket and Real Kill's body?" Papa asked the sheriff.

"Real Kill? He's dead?"

"Yes, Real-Real Kill is dead. He-he drowned last night. His body is in the last boat," Papa said.

"Well, that makes two folks dead now. Walter Townes who lived over in Occoneechee Neck drowned last night too," the sheriff reported.

Mr. Thomas came running over to Papa.

"Stanbury, how did the animals make out? Did they all survive? Is the tobacco still standing?"

He ain't been in the Low Meadows one time since Mr. Bro. Wiley died but he had the nerve to be asking about cows and 'bacco.

"Real Kill is dead, Mr. Thomas. A man is dead. We've lost another Low Meadows man."

Not one time did Papa step on his words.

"We missed you at the sittin' up last night," Miss Lottie Pearl said. For the first time in my life, I was glad she put her nose in someone else's business. Mr. Thomas just ignored her, but she wasn't letting it go for nothing in the world.

"I said we missed you at the sittin' up last night," she shouted.

Before Miss Lottie Pearl could finish her beef with Mr. Thomas, Mr. Gordon walked up.

"Morning, everybody. Sheriff Franklin just told me about Real Kill. The casket factory and funeral home so far down the hill that everything flooded. I don't have one casket left or a place to keep a single body. The only thing we have left is the house. Mrs. Creecy and Mrs. Gordon are making room for a few people. When they finish, they're going to the Creecys' to get that place ready too." Then he pulled the dead folk fabric back to see Baby Wiley.

"I see one good thing happened to us last night," he told Ma.

"Yes, it did," she said.

While Mr. Gordon was talking, Mr. Creecy walked up in boots almost to his thighs. "Men, let's get everyone settled the best we can," he said.

"Did you-you find any folk along the way?" Papa asked.

"Yes, we picked up the Ramseys who live on Cumbo Road. Their boats turned over. The coast guard will go back out shortly, and I'll go with them again. The Red Cross will be here first thing Monday morning with food and clothes."

Mr. Creecy leaned over and whispered something in Mr. Gordon's ear. Papa, Mr. Jabo, and the two dignified men gathered in a circle and started making plans for us. Ain't no telling what they were talking about. It's just no telling.

"Don't you worry about Mr. Bro. Wiley and Real Kill," Mr. Carter said as he and Mrs. Carter walked up. "We will find a way to help you as soon as we get the women and children fed. Take the casket and the body around the corner, so folk won't get upset. I got plenty caskets and we'll find one for Real Kill."

Pole seemed to ignore everyone as she jumped out of the boat and helped Mrs. Carter and Mrs. Taylor pass out apples and juice from the store. Sara and Pattie Mae joined in.

"Can you help me out of the boat, child?" Miss Remie asked Ralph.

She got out and started helping the womenfolk.

The menfolk kept on talking as Mr. Thomas turned red as a beet.

"What about the animals?" Mr. Thomas said again.

I wished I was a grown-up, 'cause I wanted to tell Mr. Thomas a piece of my mind. I wanted to say, "Don't you care 'bout Real Kill? Why didn't you try to come to the sittin' up last night?" I wanted to tell him that Mr. Bro. Wiley was a good man and he deserved respect, but I didn't say nothing. Ma and Papa would have taken the skin off my hide for talking back to grown folk.

"Come with me, Stanbury. I'm gonna take my boat to check on the farm," Mr. Thomas told my papa. Papa looked at that white man like he was as colored as us. No fear at all. Man to man.

"No-no, Mr. Thomas. I'm staying right here to take care of my family. I'm gonna take care of the Low Meadows folk."

Before Papa could say another word, Mr. Christian interrupted.

"Father, be quiet, for God's sake. Another Low Meadows Man is dead. We can't worry about your animals."

He was some kind of mad with his daddy.

"Take this money, Stanbury. Do what you got to do for the people in Low Meadows," Mr. Christian said as he pulled money from the bag he had been holding so tight earlier in the boat.

"No, thank you. I do appreciate the-the offer, but we will be fine." Papa said it with pride and dignity. Mr. Jabo slapped Papa on the back like he was proud of his friend.

"Well it's here if you need it," Mr. Christian said. Our neighbor seemed kind, like Miss Margie. The color of his skin vanished like the chickens that floated into Ole River the night before.

Twenty-Six

The Low Meadows were underwater a whole week. We had no choice but to live among the white folk. We ate at the same tables and slept in their beds.

They opened their fine community center for us to have extra room to sleep. Mr. Taylor gave us all the blankets he had in his store. He gave us food and clothes to wear along with the items we got from the Red Cross when they arrived early that Monday morning. Mr. Creecy made sure we got as much as the white folks got to wear and eat.

Ma didn't want to leave us but she went to live with the Gordons so that she could sleep in a comfortable bed with Baby Wiley. Mrs. Gordon took the girls home with her, including Pattie Mae. Sara went too and she didn't cry one time. Cousin Babe went home with Mrs. Creecy 'cause she was too old to sleep on the floor at the community center.

Me, Cousin Mer, Coy, and Barb Jean stayed at the community center and helped give out food each day. Of course Ralph was there working just like the men. I did my best to keep up with him as we carried boxes of food to people all over town.

"Where y'all going?" Ralph asked as we walked towards Pole and the other girls that Wednesday evening. They were carrying white bags with Red Cross written on the side.

"Stop yelling, Ralph. We want the white folks to know we got manners," she said.

"We are taking medicine and clean sheets to the nursing home for the Red Cross. And see . . . they gave us pins," Pattie Mae added.

Me and Ralph looked at the pins on their blouses.

"They sho' did. I have one too," Sara said with a smile.

"And they said we can keep these white gloves for our hard work," Pole chimed in, flashing her right hand in my face, still holding the Red Cross bag in the other one.

The girls were so happy, but I was even happier for Pole. I knew what them gloves meant to the future doctor.

They went their way, and me and Ralph went on about our business.

We worked until it was too dark to see our hands in

front of us, then we headed back to the community center. "Got something to show you," I said to Ralph that night at the center. Everyone was fast asleep except us. I reached over and gave him the slave papers.

"Good Lord," Ralph said. Then he tried his best to read the slave papers. "'In-vent-ory.'" He hadn't been to school in so long he could hardly read.

"Inventory," I said to help him.

"Mr. Bro. Wiley was not inventory. He was our friend," Ralph said.

"He was and he knew that," I assured Ralph.

Ralph thought for a minute.

"I hope he knew. These slave papers make me feel bad for him and his family," Ralph said as he looked again.

"That ain't your fault. We just got to talk to your daddy about you going back to school."

"I will as soon as we go home," Ralph said with a grin so big that he seemed my age again.

"Here, let me read to you tonight," I said. He moved closer to me on the floor. I was glad to help him and he wanted my help. I had room for another buddy, not just Pole. He had a space in his heart for me too. Ralph was always so distant, but not that night.

We fell asleep friends.

Me and Ralph continued to carry food and clothes door to door. Then we rushed to the center to work on his schooling. The Low Meadows women cooked, washed, and helped with the old folks. They had no problem working with the white women. Everybody got along real good. Even Miss Lottie Pearl.

Now she made it real clear that she was in charge of the colored folk. She told us how much we could eat every day so we didn't run out of food. Miss Florenza had on regular clothes from the white women and she looked prettier than she ever did in those red dresses. Wednesday night she cooked some cabbage that tasted way better than Miss Lottie Pearl's. Now, I kept that to myself. Miss Florenza surely became a Low Meadows woman that week and Miss Lottie Pearl never said another unkind word to the reformed sinner.

When it was time to sit down to eat each day, we used tin plates and Depression glass from different folks' houses all mixed in with Miss Remie's fine china.

The dead had to be cared for too, so Mr. Smitty, who owned the meat house filled with ice, kept the bodies all week. Reverend Hornbuckle and the deacons went from place to place to pray with folks. The good reverend seemed to have forgotten all about his coupe and fine clothes.

We sho' appreciated what the town people had done for us, but we were going home as soon as the funeral was over. Mr. Creecy and Papa had made their way to the Low Meadows on Wednesday to feed the animals that were still alive. They left the cows, but they brought Mule Bennett and our wagon back to town. We were glad to see that old mule.

Come Saturday morning, a week after the flood, we all gathered under the big oak tree on the hillside. Sandy Branch Baptist Church was still knee-deep in water, according to Mr. Creecy, and filled with mosquitoes. Slave Grave was underwater too, so the white preacher Reverend Lawson told Reverend Hornbuckle that we could use the white folks' cemetery. The Neck people went home and buried the dead man in Jackson where the water was low. Now, it was our turn to say good-bye to our people.

The Masons, including my papa, were pallbearers. They were some kind of dressed up in their black suits and their hats they borrowed from Mr. Gordon and Mr. Creecy. The sun was beating against their gold Mason pins harder than the rain that fell during the storm. As we walked up the hill, I looked at the twins, Coy, and some of the men that weren't old enough to be Masons yet. Willie had made it home that morning just in time for the funeral. Miss Lottie Pearl was some kind of glad to see her child. Pole too. I couldn't wait till he told us stories about places he'd traveled. Willie joined the younger men, who had their own sense of pride as they carried Real Kill to the hillside. That's right! The white folk let us bury Real Kill right beside Mr. Bro. Wiley.

Papa's eyes stayed on me while the women took care of Ma.

"Bean, come-come on over here and grab this casket. Help us carry your friend to his final resting place," he said.

I had to tell my feet to move as I rubbed the picture in my jacket pocket for strength. I stood in between Papa and Uncle Goat. Then I grabbed hold to the casket. We walked together like real men. Ralph winked at me as Coy motioned for him to help them carry Real Kill to his grave. Big Shot Bob was no place to be found, but us Low Meadows folks were there for his half brother.

Pole, Pattie Mae, and, yes, even Sara were flower girls. They looked nice in the white dresses Miss Lottie Pearl made. Of course, they wore their white gloves.

Miss Lottie Pearl read the obituary. Ma read the Twenty-Third Psalm the best she could, but she was some kind of broke up.

Deacon Ward said a few words.

"Let us give honor to two of our own, Mr. Bro. Wiley and Philip Brown, the boy we called Real Kill."

I do not know what the deacon said after that, because I was lost in the fact that I did not know my own neighbor's real name till that day.

When Deacon Ward finished, the womenfolk let the sinner sing a beautiful song.

"*Steal away, Jesus*," Miss Florenza sang all by herself.

"Sing, Florenza, sing," Miss Lottie Pearl said to her new friend. When Miss Florenza was done singing, she smiled at the reverend. She still hoped to be his bride someday.

With the little Reverend Hornbuckle knew about Mr. Bro. Wiley he did some preaching as the white folks joined us. The reverend let out all the fire and brimstone in him as he slammed his hand against his leg and did a kick.

"Mr. Bro. Wiley was a good man. He lived a good life and left us a good memories."

Kick.

"He loved everybody."

Slam.

Don't know about other folks but I was glad when he was done so that Mr. Creecy could have his say-so. He looked mighty fine in his black pinstripe suit.

"Well, Mr. Bro. Wiley, you lived a hundred years on this earth. You did not just live, you taught us about living and dying. You said what you meant and meant what you said. This town is sad without you and the Low Meadows will never be the same. You understood what it was to not have the right to live as a free man. You gained your freedom with the blood of your ancestors on your hands. You understood that and you taught us to understand."

Mr. Creecy looked at us real hard.

"All right now. I want you all to dry your tears. Never fear death! The same train that came for Mr. Bro. Wiley and Real Kill will be back for you. People, let today be a day we will never forget. We will not forget Mr. Bro. Wiley and we will not forget Real Kill. Real Kill was a child without a mother. A child without a family, but he had a heart of gold, just nobody to give it to. So we say good-bye to Real Kill and the old slave man. We leave here better people because they lived. Bean, would you come forth."

"Go-go ahead," Papa said like he already knew what Mr. Creecy was speaking of. I just could not believe it when I stepped to Mr. Creecy's side. A proclamation from the president. I could hardly hold the paper still as the gust of wind returned for the last time.

"Read it, son," Mr. Creecy said with a smile.

"I DECLARE AUGUST 5, 1940, MR. GEORGE LEWIS WILEY DAY IN THE TOWN OF RICH SQUARE, NORTH CAROLINA. THE FORMER SLAVE WILL BE REMEMBERED AS A GOOD CITIZEN WHO SERVED US ALL WITH HIS WISDOM AND GOOD SPIRIT FOR MANKIND. PRESIDENT ROOSEVELT," I said as everyone clapped slowly.

"Amen," they said as Pole kept on clapping. I wanted

to shout like the womenfolk do, but I pushed my chest out like the man I was becoming. I looked to the heavens. It was a fine day. Everything was going to be all right. Mr. Bro. Wiley was gone, but Papa and the menfolk would protect us just like they did in the storm. I was some kind of happy in my soul.

Baby Wiley let out a cry like he was pleased too. Then Mr. Creecy turned to Mr. Gordon and gave him a nod to take over the service.

"Thank you all on behalf of Gordon and Carter Funeral Homes," he said to remind us that white folk and coloreds had come together during the hardest of times. When the dignified man finished he told us to go home. Ma, she did some more hollering.

"Good-bye, Mr. Bro. Wiley, good-bye," she said over and over.

Papa and Uncle Goat helped her down the hill while Miss Lottie Pearl took Baby Wiley out of Miss Dora Mae's arm. At the bottom of the hill, we said good-bye to the white folk. Our new friends. At least for that day.

"Would you like for Mr. Faison to drive you home?" Miss Remie asked Ma.

"Thank you, Miss Remie, but I will stay with the Low Meadows folk." Then she climbed in the wagon with Papa and the Cofields. Sara and Miss Florenza joined us as Pole whispered girl talk to her new friend. They waved good-bye to Pattie Mae, and Cousin Braxton headed back to Rehobeth Road.

I sat beside Papa in front like a man. My heart felt lighter. Mule Bennett lifted his head like he was all better.

"Time-time to go, ole mule. Time to go," Papa said, leading the way. My eyes were on Taylor's Grocery Store. The WHITES ONLY sign was gone. I looked at Papa. He was all choked up.

"You-you see what I see, Son?"

"I see, Papa," I said, smiling at him.

"Ma," I turned to say.

"Yes, Bean?" She was busy kissing the newest member of the family on his fat cheeks. That boy sure did some growing in one week.

"When the land is dry, can we move Mr. Bro. Wiley and Real Kill down to the Slave Grave? I know Mr. Bro. Wiley would want to be with his people."

"Child, he gonna stay right where he is. He and Real Kill. Mr. Bro. Wiley joined his folk the night he went to heaven."

My heart was satisfied. We went home to the Low Meadows.

LATER ON

I often think back to the summer of 1940 and I realize how much the world changed, just like Mr. Bro. Wiley said it would.

When the land was dry, the grown folks gathered the little 'bacco Ole River didn't wash away. Ma and Baby Wiley got to stay home a whole month, just like Papa promised. Fall came and so did cotton season. Ma strapped the new one on her back and joined Papa and the others in the field. Me, Pole, Sara, and, yes, Ralph only saw them in the evening. Our hope, Mr. Creecy, kept his promise too. We stayed in school.

Miss Dora Mae and all the womenfolk sang songs and filled their sacks with cotton along with the men. Miss Moszella cut back on her eating so she could work in the fields too. Seem like Miss Lottie Pearl left the hillside a nicer woman. Mainly towards Miss Florenza, who never wore red again. Uncle Goat stopped lying and began coon hunting with Mr. Creecy, Mr. Jabo, and Papa. Mr. Gordon continued to bury the dead and helped the living become dignified. Mrs. Creecy and Mrs. Gordon came to the Low Meadows more often to teach the women how to read and be more than field hands. They asked the men to join the classes. Soon the sharecroppers could count their own money.

Two years after graduating from high school and working to save every dime, I went off to Shaw University. It was the fall of 1947. The same year white folks broke their promise and tried to hang a colored man name Buddy Bush in Rich Square, but that is another story.

I graduated with honors and went on to law school at North Carolina Central University. Pole went off to Saint Augustine's College where she graduated top in her class. Ralph finished high school and joined Willie as a porter. Baby Wiley grew into a fine young fellow who wanted to farm like Papa. He said farming was in his blood.

He learned to be a good Low Meadows man. Coy and Barb Jean went up North and Sara did too. The last we heard from First Lady Florenza Hornbuckle her daughter was modeling and married to a rich French man. Sara's mama never sold another drop of liquor and she loved being Reverend Hornbuckle's wife.

Me and my bride, Dr. Martha Rose Stanbury, traveled back to the Low Meadows for years to come. We still go down to the river to talk about old times. We stopped in town to rejoice in the fact that all the WHITES ONLY signs are gone. Then we walked up to the hillside to visit Real Kill, the town drunk, who lost his way. We talked to Mr. Bro. Wiley, who made it his life's mission to show us the way. Many things happened to us and our town because an old man who was once a slave died. His death changed us all in some way.

Author's Note

Just like Bean and Pole, my mother was raised in the little town of Rich Square, located among the lowlands of eastern North Carolina. Like all the towns in Northampton County, Rich Square is filled with communities that have unique traditions, that is to say, their own way of doing things. Sittin' ups—wakes for the dead—are one of those traditions.

You see, before Northampton received its first black undertaker, Mr. P. A. Bishop, in the early twentieth century, the white undertaker would embalm the body, but he would not keep the body at the funeral home. The colored folks would take their dead loved ones back home and place the body in their living room until the time for burial. In the early 1950s, Mr. Joe Gordon opened his funeral home and allowed our folks to respect the dead in his nice parlor. But for generations to come, people in our sleepy town continued to bring the body home that final night before the funeral. It was their way of keeping the tradition of our ancestors alive.

The custom of bringing the body home one last time would fade away over the years, but not the sittin' ups.

From my childhood I remember the sittin' ups that we attended all over Rehobeth Road, where I was born and raised. When someone died, the first thing that happened was the funeral director would come pick up the body. Mr. Gordon would leave quickly with the dead. The next day, he would return with the white flower of death to hang on the door. The flower was a symbol to let the neighbors know that old man death had come and taken someone away from us. Mr. Gordon would also leave lots of chairs to place around the house for the coming guests to sit in. After he made the perfect setting for the anticipated company, the crowds would gather every night for a week. The grown-ups talked about everything from who would sing the lead songs at the funeral to where the body would be laid to rest.

Despite the sad occasion, the children had a good time. We ran around, ate as many sweets as we were allowed, played games, and looked on wondering when or if a grown-up would get to crying. The shouting was exciting to us and a person fainting was like watching a good Western movie. I am so glad that I was a professional eavesdropper, because it has allowed me to pass this story of the Low Meadows and my people on to you. You see, a sittin' up really wasn't for the dead—it was for us, the living. For us to have something to hold on to. Something to laugh and cry about. Yes, the sittin' ups were for the living.

ACKNOWLEDGMENTS

Thanks to all of my angels that made this house a home! My mother, Maless Moses, and my nine siblings, Barbara, Daniel, Johnny, Scarlett Ohara, Larry, Leon, Loraine, Gayle and Jackie. I love you with all my heart!

For my sister and friends . . . Iris Moses, April Russell, Marie Showers, Wanda Linden, Stephanie Ponteau, Sandy Washington and Kim Abnatha, you all motivated me in some special way.

The progress of writing is only one step of telling a story. Thank you to Stacey Barney at Penguin and her team for the hard work you put into *The Sittin' Up*. Karen Roberts is the light of my life for each book that I write. Thanks, Karen! Thanks to Christa Heckle and all the agents at McIntosh and Otis.

My mentor Dick Gregory, you said this thing would happen. Thank you for keeping the torch burning bright for me.

And for all the folks back home that love this little girl from Rehobeth Road . . .

I love you too!